MY THERAPIST'S BOYFRIEND

EMMANUEL SIMMS

ISBN: 979-8-89379-059-7

CHAPTER 1

BEHIND CLOSED DOORS

Sunlight sifted through the blinds, striping the clinic in a soft glow. Lillian Carter leaned forward, her hazel eyes steady on Sarah. The room was hushed, save for the murmur of confessions.

"Everyone seems so sure of themselves," Sarah's voice wavered.

"Even the most confident have their doubts," Lillian said. Her words were deliberate, her tone even. Empathy shone in her gaze, not pity. "You're not alone in this."

Sarah's hands unclenched. She breathed out, slow.

"Take that step," Lillian encouraged. "One at a time."

A knock at the door. Time had passed quickly. Sarah nodded, gathering herself, and stood to leave. Lillian offered a reassuring smile, a silent promise of progress.

"Thank you," Sarah whispered.

"Next week," Lillian replied with a nod.

The door clicked shut. A brief pause filled the space—a moment's rest for Lillian before the next session. Mark entered, his shoulders hunched, his presence diminished by unseen weight.

"Mark." Lillian's greeting was warm. She gestured to the armchair opposite hers. "Please, sit."

He sat, exhaling deeply, a man unburdening his sorrows without words.

"I lost my job," he blurted. His voice was raw, stripped of pretense.

"Tell me more," she said.

Mark's story unfolded. Despair tinged his words, painting a picture of worthlessness. Lillian listened, her face a mirror of concern.

"Your value isn't defined by your job," she said. Her voice was clear, free of hesitation.

"Doesn't feel that way," Mark muttered.

"Feelings can be deceiving." Lillian leaned in, her statement quiet but firm.

Mark's eyes lifted. There was a flicker of something there—hope, perhaps. Lillian recognized it, nurtured it with her next words.

"Let's find a path forward."

The coffee shop buzzed with the hum of afternoon chatter. Daniel Moore leaned back, his blue eyes locked on Victoria's face as she detailed the unraveling threads of her marriage.

"Everything I thought we had built together," Victoria sighed, pausing to sip her espresso, "it's like he just... pulled it all apart."

"Divorce is a complex dance," Daniel said, his voice low and soothing. "Assets, emotions—they all become intertwined."

Victoria nodded, her guard lowering under the weight of shared confidences. "And the finances," she confessed, "I never paid much attention before. Now, I'm scared I'll come out of this with nothing."

"Let me help you navigate," Daniel offered, his hand briefly touching hers with calculated warmth.

"Would you?" Hope flickered across her features.

"Of course," he replied, his smile a silent vow of protection.

Lillian Carter closed the door behind Mark, turning to face her office once again. The sunlight had shifted, the lattice on the carpet now stretched and faded. Emily stood in the doorway, her eyes red-rimmed, her hands clasped tightly together.

"Emily, come in," Lillian said, her voice a gentle anchor.

Emily moved across the room, sinking into the cushioned chair like it was a life raft. "It's been six months," she began, "and it still feels like the morning I found him."

"Tell me about that morning," Lillian urged, her own voice steady.

Emily recounted the piercing silence of the house, the cold stillness of his body, the shattering realization that she was alone. Words tumbled out, each memory a shard of glass.

"Right now, those memories are sharp," Lillian acknowledged, "but with time, they will dull. Not disappear, but become less cutting."

"Is that even possible?" Emily whispered.

"It is," Lillian affirmed. "We'll work on it together."

"Okay," Emily breathed. There was trust in that single word. Trust and the barest hint of relief.

Lillian leaned back in her chair, the clock on the wall ticking a soft accompaniment to her thoughts. She glanced at the empty room, its corners now draped in the quiet of midday. The sessions from the morning clung to her like residual perfume—Sarah's anxiety, Mark's despair, Emily's grief. She closed her eyes, their stories etching into her with a weight that felt both heavy and rewarding.

She stood, stretching limbs cramped from hours of stillness. The office, usually buzzing with the energy of shared confidences, lay silent. Lillian walked to the window, parting the blinds just enough to let in a stream of sunlight. It cut across the desk, turning dust motes into swirling galaxies. A smile touched her lips. She was helping them, each one. They were moving forward.

A picture of Daniel rested on the corner of her desk. His blue eyes seemed to follow her movement, his smile a promise of solace. How was his day unfolding? He'd be at some gathering, she supposed, charming the crowd as he always did. Lillian shook her head, a chuckle escaping her. No need to worry; Daniel knew his craft.

Across town, Daniel wove through the art gallery with a practiced ease. His laughter mingled with the low hum of conversation, his nods measured, his handshakes firm. Art hung on every wall, bold and provocative, but it was the people he studied—their faces, their gestures, the subtle tells of ambition and desire.

"Your work is intriguing," said a man with a silver tie clip. "I heard about your last documentary."

"Thank you," Daniel replied, his voice a blend of humility and pride. "That was just the beginning."

"Is that so?"

"Indeed." Daniel's gaze held the other's, confident. "There's more to come. Stories that need telling."

The man's eyes flickered with interest. Daniel noticed, storing it away like currency. He had plans, and this dance of words and impressions was just another step toward them.

The clock on the wall ticked steadily, marking the end of

another session. Lillian glanced at it as she ushered Sarah out with a warm smile and words of encouragement. She straightened the cushions on the chair opposite her desk, preparing for her final appointment of the day.

Rachel stepped into the clinic, her eyes downcast, shoulders hunched in a defensive posture. Lillian offered a gentle nod, her face an open book of welcome. "Come in, Rachel. Let's talk."

The room embraced them both, a cocoon fashioned from soft lighting and the quiet hum of the air conditioner. Rachel sank into the chair, fingers knotting together in her lap. Lillian observed, her gaze never probing, always patient.

"Today feels tough," Rachel began, her voice barely above a whisper.

"Tell me about it," Lillian said. Her pen paused over the notepad, ready but unobtrusive.

"Mirror's my enemy. I just—can't see what others claim they do."

"Mirrors reflect more than we sometimes want to see," Lillian offered gently. "But they don't show everything. They can't show your courage in being here."

Rachel exhaled, a shuddering breath that seemed to carry the weight of her self-doubt. "I try to tell myself... I'm more than a reflection."

"Good." Lillian's affirmation was simple, direct. "You are. Keep challenging those thoughts."

The session unfolded, a tapestry woven from Rachel's pain and Lillian's careful guidance. Time trickled by until they reached the hour's end, and Rachel left carrying a seedling of hope, a notion to nurture against the cold glass of her unforgiving mirror.

Alone now, Lillian leaned back in her chair, the fabric sighing beneath her. The fading sunlight cast long shadows across the floor, the day drawing to a close. She thought of the faces that had come through her door, the stories spilled across the carpet like rays of light through the blinds.

She felt the ripple of their struggles, the tremors of their breakthroughs. Each client's step forward, however small, marked a victory in Lillian's heart. They were moving mountains within themselves, grain by grain, and she was their witness, their scribe.

Closing the clinic, Lillian wrapped her scarf around her neck, the fabric soft against her skin. Thoughts of Daniel fluttered through her mind, anticipation quickening her pulse. Tonight, they would share the day's victories and woes, entwined in each other's company.

He would listen, his blue eyes reflecting her stories, his presence a balm to the day's exertions. She imagined his laughter, the way it could fill a room, chase away the last tendrils of her clients' sorrows still clinging to her.

Lillian locked the door behind her, stepping out into the cool embrace of the evening. The promise of Daniel's warmth waited at home, and with it, the comfort of routine and the simple joy of shared solitude.

Daniel leaned against the polished mahogany bar, the clink of glasses punctuating the hum of conversation around him. Mason Harper stood opposite, his glass raised in a silent toast to an unseen audience.

"Latest project got greenlit," Mason said, his voice smooth as the whiskey in his hand.

"Congratulations," Daniel replied, the word sharp, a bullet shot from a gun. "I've got something in the works, too. Big names attached."

The lights of the bar flickered, casting their dance on the

bottles lined like soldiers on the shelves. Mason's eyes narrowed, a challenge simmering beneath.

"Big names mean big expectations," he countered.

"Expectations I intend to meet," Daniel shot back.

A waitress passed by, her tray laden with promise, and Daniel ordered another round. The alcohol wasn't enough to quench the envy that flared within him.

Meanwhile, Lillian turned the key, the click of the lock severing her day from the night ahead. She stepped into the chill, each breath a cloud disappearing into the darkening sky.

Her thoughts wandered to Daniel, his laughter echoing in her mind, a melody she yearned to hear. She walked, her pace steady, the rhythm a march toward the evening they would share.

She imagined his face, the lines that would form around his eyes when he smiled, the way his hair would fall just so, tempting her fingers to brush it aside. Her heart held onto this image, a beacon in the night.

The city whispered around her, but Lillian only heard Daniel's voice in the quiet spaces between.

Back at the bar, Mason's phone buzzed, the glow highlighting the smug tilt of his lips.

"Another deal, just now," he declared, almost nonchalant.

"Good for you," Daniel said, his smile not quite reaching his eyes. He clinked his glass against Mason's, the sound empty of victory.

Lillian reached her car, the metal cool under her fingertips. She slid inside, the seat embracing her gently. She started the engine, the purr a lullaby9 - 10

, the purr a lullaby coaxing her thoughts back to Daniel.

She drove, the streets emptying as the night claimed its dominion. Lights blurred past, each one a fleeting moment that brought her closer to him.

Daniel watched Mason's departing figure, his own reflection staring back at him from the darkened windowpane. He straightened his jacket, a suit of armor against the slings of ambition. His mind plotted, even as his hand waved for the check.

"Keep it," he said to the bartender, his voice smooth as the whiskey he left untouched.

Lillian parked, the familiar hum of the neighborhood wrapping around her like a well-worn shawl. She stepped out, her heels clicking a steady beat against the pavement, a testament to the day's work done.

She reached the door, her sanctuary just beyond. She paused, a deep breath drawing in the night, savoring the anticipation of Daniel's arms, his scent, the promise of their shared solitude.

The key turned, the sound a prelude to the evening's symphony. Her heart swelled with love and gratitude for the man who awaited her, the darkness beneath his charming exterior an unknown shadow she had yet to see.

Daniel surveyed the table, each dish placed with precision. Silverware aligned. Glasses gleamed under the soft light. He adjusted a napkin, folding it into a neat triangle. The table was a still life, a curated image of domestic bliss.

He checked the oven, the scent of roasted garlic and thyme wafting into the room. A corner of his mouth lifted. This was another performance, one he'd mastered. His thoughts moved, quicksilver, through the next steps of his plan. He poured wine, the ruby liquid catching the light, and stood back to admire his handiwork.

The key turned in the lock, and Lillian entered. She inhaled, the smells of dinner greeting her. Her shoulders dropped, tension melting away. She found Daniel, his blue eyes reflecting something she read as love.

"Daniel," she said, her voice soft with relief. "This looks amazing."

He crossed the space between them, smiling. "Welcome home."

They embraced, her head fitting just below his chin. She closed her eyes, breathing him in. Safe. Loved. Unaware of the game board he laid out in his mind where every piece was another move towards a checkmate only he could see.

They sat at the table, plates of food between them. Lillian's laughter mingled with the clink of cutlery. Daniel's eyes never left her face. He nodded as she spoke of victories small and large, her clients' lives unfolding in her words.

"Mark finally opened up today," she said, her hands moving as she talked. "It's like he saw himself, really saw himself, for the first time in years."

"Change is a powerful thing," Daniel replied, his voice smooth as the wine he poured.

She sipped, the red liquid bold against her lips. "And Emily," she continued, "she shared memories of her husband. I think she's starting to heal."

"Strength comes from pain sometimes," he said, storing every detail, each one a potential lever.

The meal moved along, stories and wine flowing. She did not see the wheels turning behind his gaze or the careful construction of his replies. She only heard support, felt love.

Dinner plates cleared, they stood, a silent agreement passing between them. Their hands touched, fingers interlacing. They moved to the bedroom, the space familiar and charged with a new energy.

Clothes fell away, fabric whispering to the floor. They came together, urgency in every movement. His hands traced the lines of her body, knowing each curve. She closed her eyes, lost in the sensation, the trust she placed in him complete.

"Daniel," she breathed, her voice a thread woven through the darkness.

He answered without words, their bodies speaking a language older than deceit. But even as she surrendered to the moment, his mind played out scenes yet to come. Her trust, a tool; her love, a weapon he wielded with precision.

Yet, in the tangle of limbs and whispered promises, there was something real, something that even Daniel couldn't name. It flickered in the depths of his eyes, a flame resisting the cold wind of his plans.

They lay together, breaths slowing, the night heavy around them. Lillian's heart beat a steady rhythm of contentment against his chest, while his thoughts raced ahead to futures she had yet to dream.

Lillian nestled closer to Daniel, the warmth of his body a tender cradle. Their chests rose and fell in a silent symphony, whispers of air that spoke of life's simple continuance after passion's blaze. She listened to his heartbeat, steady and sure beneath her ear—a rhythm grounding her to this moment.

"Stay with me," she murmured, half-asleep, her words barely parting the quiet room.

"Always," he replied, his voice low, a soft brush against the canvas of night.

His arm tightened around her, a secure band of flesh and intention. Lillian's mind painted futures in vibrant strokes—weddings, laughter, clients healed by her care. Each image a building block of the world she yearned to construct with him.

In the cocoon of their bed, dreams began to weave through her consciousness. Dreams of children with hazel eyes and dimpled smiles, of holidays wrapped in joy, of anniversaries marked by the gentle etching of age together. Dreams undisturbed by the shadows that clung to the edges of reality, where Daniel's true self lurked, veiled and vigilant.

Outside, the world held its breath, the dark hours holding sway. Inside, Lillian's breathing slowed, deepened, her body yielding to sleep's embrace. The city's pulse faded to a distant thrum, irrelevant to the sanctity of their sanctuary.

Daniel lay still beside her, his gaze on the ceiling, sharp and calculating. Plans spun behind his eyes like webs, delicate and deadly. Yet as he watched her sleep, a fissure of something unbidden tethered him to the present.

The night stretched on, Lillian's dreams a tender veil against the coming dawn. In her slumber, she reached for him, fingers grazing his arm in a quest for closeness. He remained motionless, the architect of facades, even as part of him longed to succumb to the genuine peace she offered.

But the night was his ally, cloaking the truth in its obsidian folds. And as Lillian drifted deeper into dreams, the darkness whispered its secrets to Daniel alone.

CHAPTER 2

CROSSING PATHS

Carla's hands shook, a visible tremor that matched the quiver in her voice. "He left without warning," she said, the words catching in her throat. "One day we're planning our future, the next he's gone with half of everything."

Lillian leaned forward, her presence a quiet anchor in the storm of Carla's grief. Her gaze never wavered from the woman before her, her own struggles tucked away behind a professional veneer.

"Everything I thought I knew, it's like it never existed," Carla continued, her green eyes fierce despite the sheen of tears that threatened to fall. She pushed a strand of blonde hair back, her movements deliberate. "I need to find my footing again, stand on my own."

"Good," Lillian said, her voice steady. "You're starting to see the path ahead."

Carla nodded, her lips pressed into a thin line, a soldier bracing for the next battle. "I will not let this break me," she declared, a spark of the old determination flaring within her.

"Carla, you're not walking this path by yourself," Lillian said, her voice a soft undercurrent in the calm of her office. "Others have been where you are."

Carla met Lillian's steady gaze, finding an anchor in the hazel depths. "It doesn't feel that way."

"Isolation," Lillian noted, "is the mind's trickery. Reach out, connections await."

A faint smile tugged at Carla's lips. "It's hard to imagine."

"Imagine, then step," Lillian encouraged. "One day, one connection at a time."

Across town, the door to the bar swung open. Daniel stepped inside, the dim lighting casting shadows that played upon his sharp features. His blue eyes cut through the haze, scanning.

There, a solitary figure perched at the bar: Kevin. His shoulders slumped, a glass cradled between weary hands. The brown eyes, once lively, now echoed cavernous depths of solitude.

Daniel moved, a predator in plain sight. He took a seat, unnoticed yet, and watched. Kevin's gaze lingered on his drink, lost in the reflection of his own downturned face.

The clink of glass against wood punctuated the silence between them, a wordless signal in the cacophony of despair that hung over the room like stale smoke.

Daniel slid onto the stool next to Kevin, the space closing with practiced ease. He leaned in, a casual tilt of his head toward the man whose loneliness hung like a worn coat.

"Rough day?" His voice was smooth, the words light but layered with intent.

Kevin glanced up, his eyes briefly meeting Daniel's before retreating back to his glass. "You could say that," he murmured.

"Mind if I join you?" Daniel's smile didn't waver, though it never quite reached his eyes.

"Suit yourself," Kevin said, a half-hearted shrug lifting his shoulders. The invitation was as empty as the seat had been.

"Thanks." Daniel signaled the bartender, ordered a drink with a nod. No need for words when gestures sufficed.

They sat in silence, sipping their drinks. The bar noise swelled around them—laughter, clinking glasses, the scratch of pool cues —yet they remained within their bubble of quiet.

"Name's Daniel," he finally offered, extending a hand not in greeting but as an anchor.

"Kevin." A handshake, firm but fleeting.

"Life has a way of throwing punches," Daniel said, setting down his glass. He watched Kevin, waited.

"Doesn't it just?" Kevin's response came with a sigh, a release of pent-up air that carried more than carbon dioxide. It bore weight —the gravity of heartbreak.

"Care to talk about it?" Daniel's tone threaded through the question, a lifeline disguised as curiosity.

"Long-term relationship ended," Kevin admitted, the words spilling as if the dam of his resolve had cracked. "Thought we were solid. Turns out, I was the only one."

"Sorry to hear that," Daniel replied, masking the strategic delight behind synthetic sympathy. "Takes courage to open up."

"Maybe." Doubt tinged Kevin's concession. He seemed to consider whether bravery or foolishness spurred his confession.

"Courage," Daniel affirmed, his gaze steady, inviting trust. "It's what brings us back from the edge, right?"

Kevin nodded, a slight dip of his head. "Hope so. Feels like a long way back, though."

"Understandable." Daniel's acknowledgment was a lure, coated in the semblance of camaraderie.

"Guess everyone's got their battles," Kevin said, a trace of solace threading through his resignation.

"True enough." Daniel raised his glass in a silent toast to shared struggles, unseen victories. "To battles and the strength to fight them."

Their glasses touched, the sound crisp in the muted din. Kevin's lips curved upward—a ghost of a smile, perhaps the first step toward something resembling hope. Daniel noted it all, cataloguing each nuance, each crack in Kevin's armor.

"Strength," Kevin echoed, the word less certain on his tongue.

"More than you know," Daniel assured, his confidence a veneer that promised sanctuary.

In the warm glow of the bar, two men drank to invisible scars. One sought solace; the other, a soul to ensnare.

"Carla," Lillian said, "take each day as it comes. Set small goals." She leaned forward, hands clasped together. "Maybe a walk in the park, or coffee with a friend?"

"Simple things?" Carla's voice wavered.

"Exactly. They build your strength back."

"Okay." Carla nodded, her eyes showing the first glint of resolve.

"Find something every day that's just for you," Lillian added. "A book, a song, anything that feels like a piece of the world is still yours."

"I can try that," Carla replied.

"Good." Lillian offered a soft, supportive smile. "Let's start there."

Across town, Daniel tilted his head, feigning concern. "You know, Kevin," he said, "sometimes what we need is to just jump back into life. No hesitation."

"Isn't that risky?" Kevin frowned.

"Risk shows us we're alive." Daniel's hand found Kevin's shoulder, a firm, reassuring grip. "You've got to trust again at some point."

"Suppose so," Kevin murmured, taking another sip of his drink.

"Start small. Talk to someone new, like now." Daniel's lips twitched upward. "See? Not so bad."

"Feels strange, though," Kevin admitted.

"Strange is good. It's the first step to finding your new normal." Daniel's advice was honeyed poison, aimed to disarm.

"New normal," Kevin repeated, pondering the phrase as if it were a lifeline.

"Exactly." Daniel patted Kevin's back and stood up. "And remember, I'm around if you need a push."

"Thanks, Daniel." Gratitude tinged Kevin's voice, unaware of the trap being set.

"Anytime, my friend." Daniel's words were smooth, a practiced melody. He left the bar, leaving behind a man clinging to hope, not seeing the web woven around him.

Carla leaned forward, her hands clasping together on the coffee-stained table that separated her from Lillian. The therapist's last phrase lingered in the air between them, a beacon in Carla's stormy sea of emotions.

"I will," she said, her voice firmer than it had been at the start of their session. "I'll reclaim what's mine. My life, my choices." Her green eyes sparked with newfound resolve, reflecting the flicker of hope that Lillian's guidance had ignited.

"Good." Lillian nodded, her hazel eyes steady, witnessing the transformation. "One step at a time."

Across town, Daniel's blue eyes never left Kevin's face, his gaze as sharp as a hawk's. He noted the slump of Kevin's shoulders, the weary tilt of his head. Vulnerable prey, ripe for the plucking.

"Loneliness can be crippling," Daniel murmured, leaning closer, invading Kevin's space with the precision of a practiced predator. "But I'm here for you, mate."

"Thanks," Kevin replied, his brown eyes clouding with a cocktail of hope and uncertainty. "It's hard to know who to trust these days."

"Trust is earned," Daniel said, his voice low and convincing. "Let me earn yours."

Kevin nodded slowly, the seeds of doubt sprouting within him. Daniel's false promises took root, twining around Kevin's judgment, threatening to choke whatever wary instincts remained.

"Everyone needs a friend," Daniel continued, the words smooth, laced with dangerous intent. "And I'm offering."

Carla leaned forward, her hands clasped as if to hold the pieces of herself together. Lillian mirrored the posture, bridging the gap with more than just words.

"Strength isn't the absence of fear," Lillian said, "it's moving forward despite it."

Their gazes locked, two souls recognizing the shared battle against invisible enemies—despair, doubt. Carla's nod was slight but spoke volumes. She wasn't alone, and that knowledge was a shield, perhaps even a sword.

"Thank you," Carla whispered.

In the dim light of the bar, Daniel watched Kevin trace the rim of his glass, a man adrift in his own life. Daniel's words were hooks, each one embedded deeper into Kevin's psyche.

"Everyone feels lost at times," Daniel said. His voice was a soft balm, but his eyes were cold steel. "It's finding our way back that defines us."

Kevin swallowed, his throat working against the weight of isolation. "I don't even know where to start."

"Start by trusting someone who wants to help." Daniel's hand landed on Kevin's shoulder, a false anchor thrown with precision. "Trust me."

A smile ghosted across Kevin's face, the first flicker of trust taking hold. Daniel's smile in return was a hunter's grin, unseen and full of dark promise.

Lillian rose, her movements sure and graceful. She rounded the desk, coming to stand beside Carla. "Time's up for today," she said. Her voice held a steady timbre.

Carla looked up, meeting Lillian's gaze. The therapist's eyes were pools of quiet strength.

"You're making strides," Lillian offered, her smile not just an expression but a message. "Remember, small steps."

"Feels like I'm climbing a mountain," Carla replied, a faint smile breaking through.

"Mountains are climbed one step at a time." Lillian's hand found Carla's shoulder, squeezing gently. "I'm here with you."

"Thanks," Carla said, standing, her own posture mimicking the strength she borrowed from Lillian.

Across town, the bar hummed with low conversations and clinking glasses. Daniel stood, his back to Kevin. His gesture was casual, a man comfortable in his skin.

"Take care, Kevin," Daniel said, his voice smooth as the whiskey on the counter.

Kevin nodded, his brown eyes wide with newfound hope. "Will

I see you again?"

"Count on it," Daniel assured him, the lie easy, his blue eyes giving nothing away.

He turned, leaving Kevin to his thoughts, the promise hanging in the air—a lifeline or a noose. The door closed behind Daniel with a soft click.

Lillian locked her office door, the click a punctuation to the day's work. Her steps were measured as she descended the stairs, each one a deliberate descent from professional caregiver to just Lillian, the woman with her own complexities. The evening air brushed against her face, cool and indifferent. She pulled her coat tighter around her and started the walk home.

Her mind replayed the sessions, the breakthroughs, and the setbacks, but mostly Carla's final, hopeful look. It was a good day's work. A difference made, she hoped.

A few streets over, Daniel merged with the crowd, his stride confident. Night had fallen like a curtain, stars hidden behind city lights. He blended in, another face among many, yet apart. His mind was not on the passersby or the buzz of nightlife. It was calculating, turning over Kevin's words, finding angles, planning moves.

The city moved around them both, uncaring and relentless. Lillian reached her apartment, her key slipping into the lock with a familiar ease. Inside, she shed her professional armor, the quiet apartment embracing her solitude.

Daniel turned a corner, his path taking him further into the night. His phone vibrated, a message lighting up the screen. He read it, thumbed a reply, and slipped the device back into his pocket. Another step taken on a path she wouldn't see until too late.

They moved through their separate lives, their choices weaving a tapestry neither could see yet. Them apart, the threads they pulled at bound to entangle in ways neither anticipated.

CHAPTER 3

SHADOWS OF DOUBT

Lillian's hands shook. She clasped them tight in her lap, the tremors betraying her composed façade. Her office, usually a sanctuary of solace for others, felt like a shrinking cell.

"I can't seem to shake this fog," she said, her voice barely above a whisper. "It's like I'm wading through quicksand."

Bethany sat across from her, the lines on her face softening with concern. She leaned in, her gaze steady and unwavering on Lillian's.

"Talk to me," Bethany urged. "I'm here."

The words hung between them, simple yet weighted with meaning. Lillian's eyes met hers, and for a moment, the trembling subsided.

"It's like I'm on the edge of a cliff," Lillian continued. "And every step could send me tumbling."

"You've been there for everyone else," Bethany said. "Now it's time to let someone be there for you."

A silence settled, but it was a comforting one, filled with unspoken understanding. There was strength in Bethany's presence, a rock amidst the stormy seas of Lillian's mind.

"Thank you," Lillian murmured, finding solace in the safety of their shared space.

The espresso machine hissed, a sharp retort in the rhythm of the coffee shop. Daniel Moore sat with one leg crossed over the other, a casual lean to his posture that belied the tension in his jaw. Mason Harper, across from him, gestured broadly with a hand as he recounted his latest venture.

"Truly, it's been an incredible journey," Mason said, his voice rich with self-satisfaction. "Premieres in three cities and already talks of awards. It's all moving so fast."

Daniel nodded, the motion tight. His fingers tapped a staccato on the table, betraying his cool demeanor. He sipped his coffee, the bitterness on his tongue a fitting parallel to the taste of envy.

"Success suits you," Daniel said, each word measured.

Mason's laugh was easy, a sound that filled the space between them with a lightness Daniel could not seem to grasp. "Oh, it's just the beginning. But enough about me. What about your projects? Anything new stirring?"

"Bits and pieces," Daniel replied, his gaze fixed on Mason's animated face. The conversation felt like a chess match, each move calculated.

"Come now, I've seen your work. You've got talent," Mason pushed, unaware of the tightening grip Daniel had on his cup.

"Thank you," Daniel said flatly. He watched Mason speak, the swell of pride in the man's chest with each breath, the way his words seemed to dance off his tongue.

"Daniel, don't undersell yourself," Mason continued, oblivious to the thin line of Daniel's lips. "Your time will come."

"Of course," Daniel conceded with a forced smile, his eyes narrowing just so, a silent vow to himself that his time wasn't just coming—it was overdue.

Lillian's hand shook as she lifted the coffee mug to her lips, a small wave of the dark liquid threatening to spill over the edge. She set it down carefully on the coaster, the porcelain clinking softly against the wood of her cluttered desk. Bethany watched from across the room, her gaze steady and patient.

"I don't know," Lillian started, her voice barely above a whisper. "There are moments with Daniel when I feel like I'm just... another scene in his screenplay. Crafted, directed."

Bethany leaned in, her office chair creaking under her weight. Her eyes never left Lillian's face, reading every flicker of emotion that crossed it.

"Is he honest with you?" Bethany asked, her voice low and even.

Lillian hesitated, her hazel eyes darting away before finding the courage to meet Bethany's once more. "I thought so. But now, there's this nagging doubt. He's too perfect at times, and I fear... I fear it's all an act."

Bethany's hand reached across the papers scattered between them, her fingers warm against Lillian's cold skin. "Listen to that doubt," she said, squeezing gently. "Trust what it's telling you."

"Instincts can be wrong," Lillian countered, but the tremble in her voice betrayed her uncertainty.

"Sometimes," Bethany conceded, her thumb stroking the back of Lillian's hand in a comforting rhythm. "But they speak truth more often than not. Especially for someone who spends her days unraveling others' truths."

A tear escaped Lillian's eye, carving a clear path down her cheek. "I just don't want to be alone," she admitted, her resolve cracking.

"Alone, you won't be," Bethany affirmed, her presence an anchor. "Whatever comes, we face it together. Remember that."

The room seemed to hold its breath, the air charged with

the weight of unspoken promises and the strength of enduring friendship. Lillian nodded, a silent acknowledgment of the battle ahead, and the ally by her side.

The clink of coffee cups punctuated the hum of the trendy café as Daniel Moore watched Mason Harper with an intensity that bordered on fixation. Mason's hands animated as he spoke, a story unfolding with every gesture, luring listeners into his world—a world where success lay thick on his tongue.

"And then, the premiere in Paris," Mason was saying, "crowds like you wouldn't believe."

Daniel's cup paused halfway to his lips, the dark liquid untouched. The envy twisted in his gut, a silent serpent coiling tighter with each of Mason's words. He set the cup down, the sound sharper than intended.

"Paris is old news," Daniel interjected, leaning back in his chair, feigning a nonchalance he didn't feel. His voice was smooth, yet it carried the weight of his envy, masked as indifference. "I'm talking about Shanghai. My last project? Let's just say it broke records. Eastern markets are the future."

Mason's eyebrow arched, his hazel eyes locking onto Daniel's blue ones. There was no missing the boast in Daniel's tone, the subtle challenge threaded through his words.

"Shanghai?" Mason's smile didn't reach his eyes. "Impressive, if true. Heard whispers about that. Big numbers?"

"Whispers don't do it justice." Daniel leaned forward, elbows on the table. "It's a game-changer."

"Game-changer," Mason echoed, his smile tight, the word hanging between them like a gauntlet thrown.

"Indeed," Daniel said, and behind his casual air, his mind raced. It was a dance of one-upmanship they both knew well, each step measured, each word a calculated move on a chessboard of their own making.

The conversation flowed on, a river of ambition and thinly veiled rivalry, while outside the window, the city moved oblivious to the undercurrents within.

Lillian's hands clasped together tightly, the thin gold band on her finger cold to the touch. The room around her felt smaller, the walls adorned with credentials that echoed a silent promise of sanctuary. But within those walls, her own fears loomed large, casting shadows over the diplomas.

Her voice broke the silence, a whisper at first, growing in strength as though it too was fighting to be heard. "I'm scared, Bethany," she said, her words trembling like leaves in a storm. "The thought of being alone... it terrifies me."

Bethany leaned in, her chair creaking under the weight of her concern. Her face, etched with lines of understanding, held a softness that filled the space between them. She listened, each word from Lillian landing like a stone in still water, ripples of empathy spreading through her.

Tears pooled in Lillian's hazel eyes, spilling over and tracing a path down her cheeks. She spoke of happiness, a thing she chased like a setting sun, always on the horizon but never within grasp. Her voice carried a resolve, fragile yet unyielding, as if saying the words could make them true.

"Your fear," Bethany said, her tone even, "it doesn't define you." Her hand found Lillian's, their fingers weaving together in a tapestry of shared strength. "You're more resilient than you know."

Lillian's gaze lifted, meeting the dark pools of Bethany's eyes. There was truth there, a beacon in the fog of her doubts. "I want to believe that," she replied, the corners of her mouth daring a hopeful smile.

"You can," Bethany assured her, her voice a steady drumbeat against the storm of Lillian's worries. "You're not alone, not now, not ever."

In the quiet office, surrounded by books that held stories of healing, Lillian found an anchor in Bethany's words. The air seemed easier to breathe, the weight on her chest lighter. And for a moment, the possibility of happiness didn't feel quite so far away.

Daniel shifted in his chair, the clink of his coffee cup on the saucer punctuating the silence. Across from him, Mason's story of triumphant box office numbers hung in the air, thick with Daniel's unspoken envy. He took a breath, let it out slow.

"Your latest, 'Eclipsed Fate', that's quite the talk around town," Daniel interjected, his voice smooth as he redirected the conversation away from his own fabricated tales. "Must be a thrill to see your vision come to life."

Mason's lips curved into a cautious smile, the glint in his hazel eyes dimmed with suspicion. He leaned back, arms crossed, the steam from his espresso curling between them like a barrier. "It's doing well. Audience seems to connect with it," he said, his tone measured.

"Yeah?" Daniel propped his elbows on the table, feigning enthusiasm. "Got to be more than just luck, right? What's your secret?"

A moment passed, filled only by the distant sound of milk being frothed and the murmur of patrons lost in their own worlds. Mason tapped a rhythm on his armrest, considering his words. "No secret, really. Just hard work and maybe a bit of timing," he finally offered, downplaying the success he wore like a second skin.

"Timing's everything," Daniel agreed, nodding slowly. His gaze lingered on Mason, reading the careful facade. The lies he had spun earlier felt heavy on his tongue now, sour and unwelcome.

"Indeed," Mason said, his guarded posture relaxing ever so slightly. "Speaking of which, how's your current project shaping up?"

The question loomed, waiting for Daniel to weave another web. But the weight of his deceit anchored him to a rare truth. "It's moving," he replied, terse and noncommittal. "You know how it is. Ups and downs."

"Of course," Mason said, his voice light but eyes sharp, missing nothing. They both knew the dance well, each step and turn an echo of ambition and rivalry.

They sipped their coffee in a truce of sorts, the battlefield quiet for now. Daniel's mind raced with plans, his charm a shield against the onslaught of his own fabrications. And in the silence, the war of wits continued, unspoken but ever present.

Lillian inhaled, her chest expanding with the breath she held like a promise. She released it slowly, each molecule of air carrying away fragments of her trepidation.

"I need to do this," she said, her words slicing the stillness of the small office. "I have to confront Daniel."

The late afternoon sun filtered through the blinds, casting striped shadows that marched across her desk. They seemed to Lillian like prison bars, reminders of the confinement she felt within her own life, her own mind.

Bethany watched her, eyes steady and sure. "You're stronger than you know," she offered, voice firm. Her hand reached out, fingers wrapping around Lillian's with a solidity that was grounding.

"Confronting him won't be easy," Lillian admitted, her gaze locked on their intertwined hands. "But I can't live with these doubts, this fear of deceit."

Bethany's thumb brushed over Lillian's knuckles. "Fear is a common companion," she said. "But it doesn't get to make the decisions for you."

"Perhaps he's innocent," Lillian mused, but the conviction behind her words was thin, brittle.

"Maybe," Bethany conceded. "But you deserve honesty. Transparency."

"Exactly." Lillian's nod was determined, her hazel eyes catching a spark of resolve. "I need to know where I stand."

"You stand with people who care," Bethany reminded her, squeezing her hand once more. "You won't face this alone."

Lillian met her friend's gaze, finding an anchor in the unspoken pledge between them. Together, they would peel back the layers of Daniel's charm, seeking the truth nestled beneath.

Daniel extended his hand, the lines in his face tightening as he did so. Mason's grip was firm, confident. The air between them charged with unspoken rivalry.

"Take care, Mason," Daniel said, his voice even, betraying nothing of the tumult inside him.

"Always a pleasure, Daniel," Mason replied, his smile not quite reaching his eyes.

Daniel watched Mason leave, the click of his shoes on the tile echoing in the now silent space. He turned back to his espresso, the crema dissolving into the dark liquid like his composure into the afternoon.

He had spun stories, woven a tapestry of successes that only existed in the words that left his lips. Now the weight of those fabrications settled on his shoulders. Lillian. Her name flickered in his mind, a candle threatened by a growing storm.

She was getting closer, her questions more pointed, her gaze more discerning. Daniel could feel the shift in her, an undercurrent that threatened to sweep away the foundation he had carefully laid.

He needed to think, to plan. His charm had always been his weapon, but Lillian's intuition was sharpening, and it was only a matter of time before she cut through the veil.

His pulse quickened at the thought. Losing control was not an option. He had to steer this narrative.

"Another coffee?" the barista asked, pulling him from his reverie.

"No, thank you," Daniel replied, standing up. He forced a curve at the corners of his mouth, a hollow mimicry of a smile. "I've got work to do."

CHAPTER 4

WEB OF DECEIT

Carla Jenkins sat in the corner of Lillian's therapy office, her figure curled into the embrace of a plush armchair. Light filtered through gauzy curtains, casting shadows that played upon her features, etching her sorrow in the quiet room. Her fingers picked at the seam of a cushion, betraying a restless turmoil beneath her still exterior.

The door hinge gave a soft squeak, and in walked Daniel Moore. His entrance cut a sharp contrast to the somber mood that clung to Carla like a second skin. He moved with an ease that filled the space, his presence undeniably magnetic.

"Rough day?" he asked, his voice smooth, eyes locking onto hers with an immediacy that seemed practiced, yet sincere.

Carla nodded, words lodged behind the tightness in her throat. She offered a half-smile, an attempt at politeness that felt foreign on her lips.

"Mind if I sit?" Daniel gestured toward the seat across from her, not waiting for an answer before taking it. The chair did not protest under his weight, nor did he shift to find comfort. He simply belonged there, as if molded into the setting.

"Divorce is tough," he said, tilting his head slightly, his blue eyes fixated on her with what appeared to be genuine concern. "But you're not alone."

Carla blinked slowly, allowing herself a moment's reprieve in his gaze. It was strange, this feeling of being seen, even under the veil of her own private anguish.

"Thanks," she managed to say, her voice small. The word hung between them, simple yet laden with the weight of unshed tears and sleepless nights.

Daniel leaned forward, forearms resting on his knees, his posture open, inviting trust. "Talking helps," he continued. "Sometimes to a stranger more than anyone else."

She found herself nodding again, drawn to the idea of sharing burdens with someone unconnected to the fragments of her past life. In this sliver of time, Daniel offered a reprieve, and Carla felt the faint stirrings of gratitude amidst the wreckage of her defenses.

Carla sipped her coffee, the steam fogging her glasses momentarily. Across from her, Daniel stirred his own cup, a casual elegance in his wrist's turn.

"Sometimes," he said, "we chase what we can't have, not seeing the value in what's right in front of us."

She looked up. The park around them buzzed with life; children laughed on swings, dogs chased frisbees, yet in this chaos, she found an odd solace in his words.

"Like happiness," she ventured, her voice steadier than she felt.

"Exactly." He leaned back, eyes never leaving hers. "You've been searching for something that's already there, inside you."

"Seems hidden away." Carla tucked a strand of hair behind her ear, a nervous tick.

"Let's find it together." Daniel's offer hung in the air, wrapped in the warmth of promise.

"Okay." A smile crept onto her lips, half-hesitant, half-willing to be led into this new chapter by someone who spoke her language of loss and hope without ever having read her pages.

Carla watched a leaf twirl to the ground, its descent a quiet dance. Daniel sat beside her on the park bench, his gaze patient.

"Ever since the divorce," she started, "I feel like I'm walking on a tightrope."

"Without a safety net?" he suggested.

"Exactly." She turned to meet his eyes, finding an anchor in their clarity.

"Life's balance is tricky," he said. "The key is finding activities that ground you."

"Like what?"

"Ever tried photography?" He tilted his head. "You have an artist's eye."

She considered it. A memory of a childhood camera flashed. "I used to love taking pictures."

"Let's bring that back." Daniel's voice was soft but sure. "Capture moments that matter."

"Maybe." Her lips curved into a tentative smile, touched by the thoughtfulness woven into his words.

"Or hiking?" he pressed on. "Nature has a way of soothing souls."

"Sounds... nice." Carla's voice trailed off as she pictured winding trails and canopies of green.

"Saturday then?" Daniel asked. "There's a perfect trail not far from here."

"Okay." The word was out before doubt could take hold.

"Great." He stood up, helping her to her feet. "It's a date."

"Thank you, Daniel." Gratitude laced her words.

"Thank me after." He winked. "You might just rediscover parts of yourself along the way."

As they parted, Carla felt a flutter in her chest, an excitement for Saturday and for the man who made it seem so full of possibility.

Carla lifted her camera, the lens focusing on a burst of sunlight through the leaves. Daniel stood close, watching her frame the shot.

"Perfect," she murmured.

"Like the photographer," he said.

Carla lowered the camera, cheeks warming. Their eyes locked. Daniel's gaze intense, unwavering. She felt seen, truly seen, as if he could peer into the essence of her. It thrilled her. It scared her.

"Nature suits you," he said.

She nodded, her pulse quickening. "Makes me feel alive."

"Alive is good. After feeling numb for so long." He was quoting her, words she had spoken in Lillian's office, not knowing they would reach him.

"Exactly." She breathed out, touched by his memory, his insight.

"Let's sit," he suggested.

They found a bench beneath an oak, its branches a canopy above them. Daniel sat first, patting the space beside him. Carla joined, her side pressing lightly against his. The contact sent a current through her.

"Look at this view," he whispered.

Carla followed his gaze to the valley below, bathed in golden light. It was breathtaking.

"It's beautiful," she agreed.

"Like this moment," Daniel said, turning toward her. His hand found hers. Fingers intertwined. Her heart skipped.

"Daniel..." she began, voice trailing.

"Carla," he interrupted, "you deserve happiness."

His thumb brushed over her knuckles. It was a simple gesture but laden with intent. Carla felt herself melting into him, her resolve dissolving.

"Maybe I've found it," she admitted softly.

"Maybe you have." His lips curved into a smile that didn't quite reach his eyes.

They sat together, hands clasped, the world reduced to the space between them. Daniel leaned in, his breath warm on her cheek. Carla turned her face toward his. Their lips met, a gentle pressure, a promise of more.

"Trust me," Daniel whispered against her mouth.

"I do," Carla replied, her voice a soft echo of his own desire.

As they pulled away, her mind buzzed with a cocktail of emotions. Daniel's presence was comforting, intoxicating. And as the sun dipped lower, casting long shadows across the trail, Carla couldn't shake the feeling that she was exactly where she needed to be.

The sun had set when they left the trail, the twilight casting a cool blue veil over the world. Carla's breath came out in visible puffs as they walked in silence, her mind still replaying the warmth of Daniel's lips on hers.

"Let's get coffee," Daniel said suddenly, breaking the quiet that had settled between them.

"Sure," Carla agreed, her voice betraying none of the turmoil inside her. The idea of something warm was comforting.

They found themselves at a quaint coffee shop, its windows foggy from the heat inside. The bell above the door jangled as they entered, the sound oddly jarring in the calm evening.

"Two lattes, please," Daniel ordered, his voice smooth and sure. He paid before Carla could even reach for her purse. She smiled at him, grateful yet uneasy.

"Thank you."

"Anything for you," he said, his eyes holding hers. There was depth there she couldn't fathom.

They sat at a corner table, the latte's steam swirling between them. Carla wrapped her hands around her cup, the ceramic radiating into her skin.

"Tell me about your dreams," Daniel prompted, leaning forward.

Carla hesitated, then spoke of aspirations and hopes she hadn't voiced in a long time. Daniel listened, nodding, his gaze never leaving her face. It made Carla feel seen, understood.

"Your strength is inspiring," he said after a pause. His hand reached across the table, covering hers. "You can achieve anything."

"Even after everything?" she asked, her voice small.

"Especially after everything," he assured her, squeezing her hand gently. Carla felt a surge of confidence, a belief in his words.

Their conversation drifted to lighter topics, but Carla noticed things. The way Daniel's smile tightened when their laughter grew too loud. How his eyes darted to the door every time it opened. Little things, easy to miss.

"Let's walk," Daniel suggested once they finished their drinks. The air was crisp, the night sky clear. They strolled through the deserted streets, the silence comfortable, yet charged.

Without warning, Daniel pulled her into an alcove and kissed her. The passion took her breath away. Her back pressed against the cold brick, his body a shield from the world. His hands roamed with a possessiveness that thrilled her.

"Carla," he breathed, his voice rough with desire.

She couldn't speak, her senses overwhelmed by his closeness, his scent. But in the back of her mind, a whisper cautioned her. It went unheeded.

"Daniel," was all she managed, her hands gripping his jacket, drawing him closer.

Their passion was a living thing, wild and untamed. In that moment, nothing else mattered.

When they finally parted, Carla's heart pounded furiously. Daniel's expression was unreadable in the dark. He brushed a kiss on her forehead, a tender gesture that belied the intensity of their embrace.

"Come on," he said softly. "I'll walk you home."

Carla nodded, her thoughts a tangle of emotion and doubt. She followed him, the echo of their footsteps a steady beat in the night.

Carla's pulse still raced from the kiss when they reached her doorstep. Daniel's silhouette loomed tall against the streetlight's amber glow.

"Have you ever thought about investing?" he asked, his tone casual.

"Investing?" Carla echoed, a frown creasing her brow as she searched her keys.

"Sure. It's a way to build a future. I know a thing or two." He leaned against her door frame, arms folded, a picture of ease.

"Maybe," she said. The key slid into the lock, a metallic click in the quiet.

"Think about it," he urged. "I could help you."

"Help me?"

"Absolutely. There's this opportunity." His voice was soft, persuasive. "A start-up. Tech stuff. It's going places."

"Tech stuff," Carla repeated. She turned the handle, the door creaking open.

"Think big, Carla. This could be our chance." His use of 'our' was deliberate, inclusive.

"Ours," she whispered, stepping inside.

"Let me show you the details tomorrow?" Daniel's hand rested lightly on the door, holding it ajar.

"Okay," she said. Her heart wanted to leap at the idea of 'ours'. But her mind hesitated.

"Goodnight, Carla." He smiled and let the door close.

"Night," she murmured to the empty space.

Inside, the apartment was silent, the darkness waiting. She moved through the rooms, unease growing with each step. On the coffee table, her laptop lay open, an article about financial scams half-read.

She sat down, her fingers hovering over the keyboard. Slowly, she typed in the name of the tech company Daniel had mentioned. The search returned nothing. No website. No news articles. Just forum whispers, doubts.

"Nothing," she whispered. Her phone buzzed on the table, a

message from Daniel lighting up the screen.

"Sleep well. Dream of what we can build together," it read.

Carla's thumb hovered over the reply button. Instead, she looked back at the screen. A new search. Daniel Moore. There were too many with the name. She added 'investment'.

The top result made her breath catch. A forum post questioning a Daniel Moore involved in dubious investment schemes.

"Can't be him," she said aloud, dismissing it. But the seed of doubt had been planted.

Another buzz. An email notification. A forgotten subscription to a financial watchdog newsletter. She clicked on it without thinking.

"New Ponzi Schemes on the Rise" the headline screamed. Her eyes skimmed the text, then stopped. A familiar pattern described. A knot formed in her stomach.

"Daniel wouldn’t," she whispered. But the doubt was a worm now, eating away at her certainty.

"Get some rest," she told herself, closing the laptop. The room was dark again, the only light coming from the street outside. She stood and walked to the window, pulling the curtain aside just enough to peer out.

Below, the street was empty. No trace of Daniel. Just parked cars and the hum of a city settling for the night.

"Who are you, Daniel Moore?" she asked the reflection in the glass.

Her phone lay on the table, silent now. She looked at it, considering. Then she picked it up and opened a note app. She typed a single word: Investigate.

Her finger hovered over the 'save' button. Then she pressed it.

Her heart raced, not with desire this time, but with the thrill of the hunt.

"Tomorrow," she said to her reflection.

And then everything went black.

CHAPTER 5
TANGLED HEARTS

The grand doors swung open. A wave of jazz and chatter washed over Lillian and Daniel. She clutched her clutch, the sequins catching light like tiny stars in a fast-paced galaxy.

"Quite the spectacle, isn't it?" Daniel's voice, low and smooth, cut through the din.

"Overwhelming," she admitted.

He smiled that smile, the one that always seemed to know more than it let on. Lillian felt the familiar pull in her chest as he slipped his hand from hers and stepped into the throng.

Men slapped his back. Women leaned in, lips painted and eager. Daniel moved among them, a shepherd parting sheep. Laughter followed him, a trail of breadcrumbs that Lillian could not help but want to pick up.

From her vantage point by the entrance, she watched him. The way his head tilted when he listened, how his hand found shoulders and arms, a touch here, a nod there. Each guest bloomed under his attention, flowers reaching for sunlight.

She crossed her arms, the fabric of her dress hugging her too tightly. Jealousy, a sour note in the night's symphony, crept up her throat. It clawed at her, whispering doubts dressed as observations.

"Daniel Moore," someone exclaimed, a man with a laugh too

loud. "Always the life of the party!"

And wasn't he just? Lillian's gaze lingered, the pride she had in him wrestling with the jealousy that sought to color it dark. He was hers, wasn't he? Yet out there, amidst the glamour and the gaiety, he belonged to everyone and no one all at once.

The music swelled, a crescendo that filled the space between her thoughts. She took a step forward, then another, drawn by the invisible thread that tied her to Daniel. But she stayed at the edge, where the lights were dimmer and the faces less distinct, watching the man she loved be the man everyone loved.

Lillian leaned against a marble column, her gaze drifting across the sea of revelers. The swell of music and laughter seemed to buoy her spirits momentarily before the weight of her own unease pulled her back down. She watched as Mason Harper navigated the throng with the ease of a captain at the helm of his ship.

"Ms. Carter," Mason's voice cut through the cacophony, "your presence here honors us."

She turned, the soft light catching the kindness in her eyes. "Thank you, Mr. Harper."

"Your work," he began, lifting a glass in her direction, "it's more than admirable—it's vital. Few possess your dedication."

For a fleeting moment, her worries about Daniel dissolved into the clinking of glasses and Mason's affirming words. Her lips curled into a modest smile, a blush gracing her cheeks. "You're too kind."

"Truth, Ms. Carter. Merely truth."

Across the room, Daniel's silhouette carved itself out from the crowd. He moved with purpose towards the bar where Kevin Dawson stood, a lone figure cast adrift. A glass was in Kevin's hand, but it was his eyes that held the thirst—a longing for connection.

"Kevin," Daniel's voice was low, carrying just enough warmth to thaw the ice around the man's shoulders. "Rough night?"

"Ah, Daniel," Kevin replied, a note of relief threading through his tone. "Just not much for these things, you know?"

"Understood." Daniel leaned in, his blue eyes reflecting a practiced empathy. "Let's talk."

As they exchanged words, Lillian's attention was briefly ensnared by the spectacle of their interaction. But there was more to do, conversations to be had. She reminded herself to breathe, to remain present amidst the opulence of Mason Harper's extravagance.

"Perhaps we should discuss potential collaborations," Mason suggested, offering Lillian an opportunity she knew could not be ignored.

"Indeed," she replied, her voice steady, even as her heart continued its uneven rhythm.

Lillian watched from the fringe. Daniel's hand settled on Kevin's shoulder, a gesture that spoke of camaraderie to an unsuspecting eye. Their heads were close, words exchanged in hushed tones that were lost beneath the thrum of bass and laughter. She sipped her drink, the glass cool against her lips, and tried to grasp the thread of their conversation.

"Loneliness can be a beast," Daniel said. His voice barely carried over the music, but Lillian caught the edge of it—a soft lure.

Kevin nodded, his eyes wide and seeking. "It's been rough, I won't lie."

"Sometimes," Daniel continued, "the cure is in the poison. You ever think about that?"

Lillian tensed, her gaze narrowing. There was a dance to Daniel's dialogue, a dangerous rhythm. She could see it in the tilt of Kevin's head, the way he drank the words like they were salvation.

"Poison?" Kevin's brow furrowed, but there was intrigue behind the skepticism, a door left ajar.

"Figuratively," Daniel said with a dismissive wave of his hand. "A little risk. A walk on the wild side. It's what people are missing sometimes."

Lillian felt a prickling sensation at the back of her neck. It was not the first time she had seen Daniel weave his web, the strands invisible until you were caught. But Kevin was her client, his trust something she had nurtured.

"New experiences," Daniel pressed on, "can be... transformative."

Kevin's nod was slow, contemplative. He took a sip of his drink, eyes never leaving Daniel's face.

"Transformative," he echoed.

Lillian set her glass down quietly on the nearest table. The room spun with energy, bodies moving in sync with the beat, yet she stood still, apart. She needed to speak to Kevin, to unravel Daniel's knots before they pulled too tight. But not now, not here. The timing was everything, and the truth was a delicate thing.

She looked away, her heart thumping a warning. The night was far from over, and already it was taking unexpected turns.

Lillian edged closer to the throng, her gaze fixed on Daniel and Kevin. Daniel's hand rested lightly on Kevin's shoulder —a gesture feigning camaraderie. Daniel spoke; his voice too low for eavesdropping, yet Lillian caught the occasional word —"opportunity," "trust" —each like a stone dropped into the pit of her stomach.

"Daniel has a knack," Mason said, appearing beside her with a glass in hand. His smile was a well-practiced curve. "He can sell sand in the desert."

"Can he?" Lillian replied, her words clipped.

"Indeed." Mason raised his glass as though toasting to some private joke. "Come, they're discussing a project I'm developing. Your insights as a therapist could be invaluable."

She hesitated, torn between the pull of professional intrigue and the knots of suspicion tightening around her heart. She followed nonetheless, her steps measured. The crowd parted for Mason Harper. They always did.

"Ah, Lillian," Daniel greeted her without missing a beat. "We were just talking about human behavior—how it drives our stories."

"Is that so?" Lillian kept her voice neutral. A part of her rebelled against the idea of aiding this conversation, of being a pawn in whatever game Daniel played.

"Absolutely," Mason chimed in. "Films need authenticity, and what's more authentic than the human psyche?"

"Quite," she murmured. Her eyes met Daniel's, searching for a flicker of truth. All she found was the blue ice of calculation.

"Your thoughts, Lillian?" Daniel asked, tilting his head slightly.

"Sometimes," she began, feeling the weight of their attention, "the most authentic actions are those we regret."

"Regret," Mason mused. "That's a powerful theme."

"Indeed," Lillian agreed, her mind not on film projects but on the scene unfolding before her—the real drama, the one where consequences were not scripted and the actors bled true.

Daniel leaned in, his voice a low hum that commanded the space around him. "Mason, the key is in the details, the tiny mannerisms that reveal character."

"Go on," Mason urged, captivated.

"An actor must become the vessel for those quirks, embody them until they're indistinguishable from the role."

Lillian watched, her heart a pendulum swinging between admiration and dread. Daniel was a silhouette cut sharply against the backdrop of opulence, every gesture deliberate, each word a crafted note in the symphony of his deceit.

"Interesting," Mason said, his eyes reflecting a spark of competitive fire.

Lillian's gaze drifted. Across the room, Kevin shifted weight from one foot to the other. He took a breath, then another, before stepping towards a woman with laughter spilling from her lips like wine from an uncorked bottle.

"Acting is truth," Daniel continued, "and truth is often uncomfortable."

"Exactly," Mason nodded, not seeing the play unraveling beyond their circle.

Lillian's fingers tightened around her glass. She felt the chill of the crystal against her skin, a cold reminder of the fragility of trust. Kevin reached out, his hand almost touching the woman's arm, and Lillian's breath caught. She knew that courage came at a price—one she feared Kevin could not afford.

"Daniel," Lillian interjected, her voice a thread weaving through the air. "Perhaps we should consider how our actions ripple outwards."

"Life is a series of ripples," Daniel replied, his smile never reaching his eyes. "Isn't it?"

"Perhaps," Lillian conceded, watching as Kevin's ripple touched the shore of another's world, the outcome yet unknown.

Lillian watched as Daniel's laughter mingled with the gilded echoes of the room. She edged closer, her resolve firming with each step. Her mind thrummed with questions, the need to peel back his veneer pressing against her tongue.

"Daniel," she began, her voice almost lost in the crescendo of surrounding chatter.

He turned, his attention swift and total. "Yes, love?"

The word hung between them, a sweetly wrapped lie. She searched his face, that well-crafted mask of concern and warmth. The words of confrontation retreated, crumbled under the weight of public spectacle.

"Nothing," she lied, tucking away her doubts like errant strands of curly hair behind her ear. "Just checking in."

"Always so caring." His smile was tender but his eyes, distant horizons.

She nodded, a silent pact to bide her time.

As the evening unspooled, Lillian's gaze found Daniel repeatedly. Each laugh, each touch on the arm from him to others, a strike to the matchstick of her wariness. She floated through conversations, her replies automatic. Her thoughts were moths to the flame of her suspicions. She watched the guests, their faces masks just like Daniel's, all hiding something. Perhaps it was just her, seeing shadows where there was only light.

Kevin laughed, the sound brittle. His companion leaned in, red lips spelling danger. Lillian's chest tightened, knowing it was Daniel's whispered poison at play.

"More wine?" A waiter offered relief in a glass.

"Thank you." She took a sip, the taste not reaching her. Her eyes stayed fixed on the tableau across the room. It was playing out, life imitating the twisted art of Daniel's advice.

"Everything alright, Lillian?" Mason's voice cut through her observation.

"Fine," she said, too quickly. "Just... thinking about a client."

"Ah, always working." He raised his glass to her dedication, oblivious to the true work unfolding before her.

Lillian excused herself, her retreat to the balcony a desperate gasp for air. The city lights blinked, indifferent stars to her inner turmoil. She had wanted to confront Daniel, strip away the layers until she found the truth or the void beneath. But not here, not with prying eyes and ears.

"Are you okay?" Daniel appeared, concern etched in the lines of his face, a perfect sculpture of empathy.

"Fine," she repeated, the word a pebble in her mouth.

"Let's enjoy the night." He pulled her close, the warmth of his body a contradiction to the chill in her heart.

"Enjoy," she echoed, her smile as brittle as Kevin's laugh.

The night wore on, the music a relentless tide against her thoughts. She danced with Daniel, moved by his lead, yet every touch reinforced the barrier between them. Her doubts were thieves, robbing her of the joy around them. And as they swayed, Lillian knew this dance was one of evasion. Her heart kept tempo with the beat, counting down to the moment when the music would stop and she'd have to face the silence.

Lillian drifted through the crowd, a ghost in a hall of laughter and light. Her eyes found Daniel again, the way he held a glass, the tilt of his head as he laughed. Simple gestures that once drew her to him now seemed foreign, practiced.

The music surged, a crescendo that mimicked the pounding in her chest. She sipped her drink, the ice clinking like a warning. The bubbles caught in her throat, a fizzy trap for words unspoken.

"Another, Lillian?" Mason's voice cut through the din, an anchor to the moment.

She nodded, handed over her empty glass. The bartender poured and she watched the liquid rise, clear and predictable. How easy it was to fill a glass, how hard to fill the spaces between people.

Daniel's arm slid around her waist, his touch a brand through the fabric of her dress. She stiffened, then relaxed into the role expected of her. They moved together, a picture of unity to the unknowing eye.

"Having fun?" His whisper brushed her ear, a feather laced with steel.

"Of course," she replied, her voice a thin veil over the chasm within.

He smiled, a magician confident in his illusion. She returned it, her own mask secure. The night unfolded, a tapestry of gaiety that mocked her solitude.

Glasses clinked, voices melded into one distant hum. Lillian stood at the heart of it all, yet apart. She turned, her gaze catching on a couple entwined in a shadowed corner, envy a sour taste in her mouth.

It was time, she knew. Time to confront the man who could hold her with a look, unravel her with a word. But not tonight. Tonight the party played on, a masquerade where truths hid behind velvet curtains.

As the laughter swelled, Lillian's resolve wavered. Doubts whispered, louder than the music, louder than her heart. She must ask, must know, but fear was a masterful opponent.

"Let's get some air," she said, pulling away from Daniel's grasp. They stepped onto the balcony, the city sprawled beneath them, uncaring. He stood close, too close.

"Is everything okay, Lily?" His voice was soft, a thread trying to weave itself back into the fabric of her trust.

She looked at him, at the face she loved, the enigma she feared. "Yes," she lied, the word a stone dropped into the well of their relationship, waiting for the splash that never came.

"Good." He kissed her forehead, a benediction or a branding, she couldn't tell which.

Back inside, the party raged. She was alone amidst the revelry, a silent scream against a symphony of ignorance. She would confront him, soon. But for now, the fear held her mute, a captive audience to a play with no clear end.

CHAPTER 6

FACADE OF LOVE

The key turned with a soft click, and the door edged open. Shadows pooled in the corners of the entryway, but the flicker of candlelight beckoned from within. Lillian paused, her handbag slipping off her shoulder. The scent of rosemary and roasted garlic wrapped around her, tugging at the edges of her fatigue.

"Daniel?" Her voice was a tentative thread in the dimness.

No answer came, only the soft hum of a melody playing somewhere beyond the hallway. She stepped inside, her pulse quickening. The dining room revealed itself, bathed in the warm glow of candlelight, each flame dancing atop slender holders. The table was set for two, silverware aligned with precision beside plates that promised a meal prepared with care.

A figure emerged, his form solidifying from the embrace of dusk. Daniel stood there, the shadows clinging to him like an old friend. His smile held secrets, lighting up his eyes in a way that drew the room's darkness into sharper focus.

"For you," he said, extending a bouquet of white lilies towards her.

Lillian took them, their petals soft against her fingers. The flowers felt heavy, laden with meaning she couldn't quite grasp. He guided her to the table, the chairs scraping gently against the wood floor. The music swelled—a violin string sighing, a piano key whispering—as if underscoring the scene.

"Sit," Daniel urged, pulling out her chair with a flourish.

She did, her movements automatic, her mind still catching up. The fabric of her chair embraced her, and she looked across the table into Daniel's gaze. Blue, clear, they held her just as firmly as any touch.

"Thank you," she murmured, her doubts momentarily retreating like the tide going out to sea.

The scent of the meal mingled with the lilies, wrapping Lillian in layers of familiarity. Daniel poured wine, the ruby liquid catching the candlelight. He raised his glass.

"To us," he said.

Her heart hummed a tentative agreement. She sipped, the warmth spreading through her. His eyes never wavered, holding hers in a silent conversation that spoke louder than words. They talked then, the food untouched as their voices filled the space between them.

"Remember Greece?" she asked.

"The stars were jealous of your eyes," he replied.

She laughed, a sound she hadn't known she'd been keeping inside. They shared stories, laughter knitting the frayed edges of her day. Her dreams spilled out, her fears tagging along, seeking to be heard. Daniel listened, his nods stitching the gaps in her confidence.

"Your strength amazes me," he said.

She reached across the table, her hand hesitating before finding his. Their fingers laced together, an anchor amidst the sea of uncertainty that had been threatening to drown her. The connection they had lost, found again in the confession of souls over candlelight.

Time slipped by unnoticed, plates cleared away, the room

growing darker as candles burned low. They moved closer, the music a distant murmur compared to the beat of their hearts. Daniel's hand traced the line of her jaw, a touch lighter than air but heavy with intent.

"Stay with me," he whispered.

Lillian answered without words, her body leaning into his. Their lips met, a collision of need and longing. The kiss deepened, hands exploring, reaffirming memories etched in the language of touch. Breathless whispers traded in the dark, each one a thread pulling them tighter together.

Their embrace was a dance of shadows, each movement stoked by the flames of desire. The world outside faded, leaving only the two of them, adrift in a sea of passion where doubts drowned and only certainty remained.

The restaurant buzzed with life, servers weaving between tables lit by the soft glow of pendant lights. Daniel leaned back in his chair, a casual tilt to his smile as he watched Carla approach. Her heels clicked a steady rhythm on the tiled floor, a metronome to her heart's uneasy tempo.

"Carla," he greeted, rising just enough to suggest courtesy. He waited for the flicker of surprise in her eyes before reaching into his jacket. "For you."

His hand emerged holding a small, velvet box. He opened it towards Carla, revealing a silver necklace, delicate and lustrous. It caught the light, throwing patterns on her face that danced like the promise of something better.

"Oh, Daniel, it's beautiful," she said, her voice a mixture of delight and disbelief.

"Nothing less for you." His words were silk, smooth and enveloping. He stood, clasped the necklace around her neck. His fingers brushed her skin, a whisper of contact. She shivered, not from cold.

They sat, menus untouched as Daniel spun his narrative. The film project was a mosaic of potential, each piece a vivid stroke of success. He spoke of directors, of scripts that held weight, of actors lined up like chess pieces on a board of prestige.

"Your vision is incredible," Carla breathed, leaning in. Her eyes reflected the candlelight and the grandeur of his tale.

"Join me in it," Daniel urged. He reached across the table, his hand a bridge. "Invest, and we rise together."

Carla's hesitation was a bird in flight, brief and destined to land. She nodded, her green eyes locked onto his blue ones, seeing only the reflection of her dreams cast back at her.

"Okay," she whispered, sealing her fate with a word. Daniel's smile did not reach his eyes, but she did not see. The truth lay hidden, a shadow cloaked by the brilliance of his deception.

The door clicked shut behind them. Carla's heels echoed against the hardwood floor, a staccato to the rhythm of their breaths. Daniel's apartment loomed, shadows and half-light. He led her in, his hand firm on her back.

"Nice place," she said.

"Thanks," he replied, his voice low.

The city lights spilled through the windows, casting a mosaic on the walls. The necklace glittered at Carla's throat, an emblem of trust, a shackle of deceit. She turned to him, her eyes searching.

Daniel smiled, his lips a curve of secrets. He didn't speak. Words were unnecessary; his intentions clear in the tightening grip, the pull towards him.

She resisted, but faintly. Her body betrayed her doubts as it leaned into his warmth. His hands traced her curves, a cartographer mapping uncharted territories with a greed for conquest. Their lips met, and the world narrowed to the space between them.

"Are you sure?" she asked.

"Absolutely," he whispered, the lie smooth as velvet.

Her surrender was silent, a nod, a closing of eyes. They moved together, a dance of need and manipulation. As they fell onto the bed, passion consumed them, blinding, devouring.

Later, he watched her sleep, her chest rising and falling with naive dreams. He stepped out, a shadow amongst shadows, leaving her in the tangled sheets—a pawn crowned queen for a night, unaware of the game played.

Lillian lay in the dark, Daniel's arm heavy around her. The room smelled of sweat and jasmine, the remnants of their shared desire. She listened to his breathing, even and deep, the cadence soothing her fraying thoughts.

Tonight had been different. His touch had been tender, his gaze seeking hers in the dim light. It felt like love, or what she imagined it should be. She wanted to hold onto this feeling, the connection that promised more than empty spaces between conversations.

"Goodnight, Lill," he murmured, his voice thick with sleep.

"Night," she whispered back, her heart aching with hope.

The candle had burned down to a stub, the light flickering out. In the darkness, Lillian closed her eyes, willing the embers of their intimacy to kindle something lasting. She breathed in the scent of him, the room, the night—holding it close, a talisman against the creeping doubts that waited just beyond reach.

Carla's eyes fluttered open. The room spun slightly, reality seeping in with the morning light. She clutched the sheets, her skin still warm from the night's embrace. Satisfaction hummed through her, but it was a discordant melody.

She sat up, the weight of unease settling on her chest. It was there, this small voice that whispered doubts she couldn't quite silence. Her gaze fell upon the empty space beside her, the imprint of a body now gone. The vulnerability wrapped around her like a shroud.

She rose, wrapping herself in a robe that felt too large. Carla moved to the window, peering out at the city that never slept. There was a tightness in her throat, an unspoken question lingering in the air. She turned away, leaving the view and her unrest standing alone.

Lillian's eyes were heavy, her body leaden against the cool sheets. Daniel's breath was steady, a quiet rhythm in the otherwise silent room. She traced the line of his jaw with a fingertip, feeling the stubble of a night passing.

His arm tightened around her, possessive even in sleep. She should have felt secure, cherished. Yet something tugged at her consciousness, a thread pulling loose. She brushed her lips against his shoulder, seeking reassurance in the familiarity of his skin.

"Always," he murmured without waking.

"Always," she echoed, the word hollow between them.

The room was stripped of pretense in the half-light of dawn. Lillian lay still, listening to the beat of her own heart. Was it syncopated with his, or was she dancing to a tune only she could hear?

Doubt crept in, a slow tide eroding the shore of her trust. She closed her eyes, willing the love she felt to be enough, to be real. But love was not a fortress; it was a veil that could be lifted, revealing truths one might never wish to see.

Carla's breath slowed, surrendering to sleep's embrace. Dreams wove through her consciousness like ribbons of light, dreams where she stood tall, basked in the glow of triumph and affection. She saw herself on an elevated stage, applause thundering around her, a figure at her side sharing the spotlight. He was blurry, a placeholder for success, not quite Daniel but not apart from him either.

Her chest rose and fell with peaceful rhythm, a stark contrast to the storm that was to come. Her lips curved in a soft smile as she danced through dreamt victories and imagined accolades. In her slumber, she was untouchable, unbowed by deception.

Across town, dawn crept into Lillian's room, its pale light casting shadows across the walls. She watched them play out silent dramas, her mind a battleground between love and suspicion. Daniel's presence was a weight, a warmth she yearned for and yet questioned. The truth loomed over them, a specter neither could see nor evade.

Lillian turned her gaze from the waking sun, from the doubts it illuminated. Her heart beat a staccato rhythm against the silence. Doubts whispered, insistent as the morning breeze that slipped through the cracks of the window.

In two separate beds, two women lay beside the same man, their lives intertwined by his carefully spun lies. Carla dreamed of futures bright and shining, while Lillian clung to the remnants of night, hoping darkness would keep the truth at bay.

The day held its breath, knowing the revelations it would bring. Neither woman could escape the web they were caught in, each strand leading back to Daniel.

CHAPTER 7

THE FIRST DOMINO FALLS

The phone rang, piercing the calm of Lillian Carter's office. She answered, heart seizing as the caller introduced himself as a police officer. Words like 'suspicious' and 'death' clung to the air around her.

"Daniel Moore's client," the officer said. "I'm afraid they're dead."

Lillian gripped the receiver tighter, knuckles whitening. Her hazel eyes darted across the room, seeking an anchor in the storm of information. She scribbled notes, each detail a heavy weight in her stomach.

"Thank you, Officer," she said, voice steady despite the tremor she felt inside. "I'll be there soon."

She hung up. The room spun slightly, reality skewing. Daniel's face flashed in her mind—those blue eyes, that confident smile. A shiver ran down her spine.

"Reassurance," she whispered to herself, a mantra to quell the rising panic. She needed to see him, to gauge his response. Daniel could dispel her fears with a word, a look. Or confirm them.

She stood, pushing back the chair with more force than necessary. Lillian walked out of her office, the corridor stretching before her like a challenge. Her heels clicked against the floor, quick and determined.

"Support," she thought, approaching Daniel's door. "Just

support."

Lillian paused at Daniel's door, the frosted glass obscuring the scene within. She pushed it open. Inside, Daniel hunched over his desk, papers sprawled like fallen leaves in an autumn storm. His pen scratched a relentless rhythm.

"Daniel," Lillian said, her voice cutting through the silence.

He looked up, a flicker of annoyance crossing his sharp features before he schooled them into neutrality. "Lillian, what is it?"

"There's been a death," she began, her gaze locked onto him, searching for a crack in the facade.

"Whose?"

"Your client."

"Ah." He returned to his papers, the pen never ceasing. "These things happen."

"Doesn't it bother you?"

"Bother me?" Daniel stopped writing, finally looking at her, though not quite meeting her eyes. "They had issues. Deep ones. It was only a matter of time."

"Only a matter of time?" Her voice rose, a note of incredulity threading through the words.

"Let's not be naive, Lillian. We see it every day."

"Naive?" Anger sparked in her, but she tamped it down, replaced by cold dread. She studied him, this man she thought she knew. The impassiveness of his face chilled her more than any lie could have done. Something was wrong. Deeply so.

"Okay," she said, backing away, her mind churning. She turned and left him to his work, the scratching of the pen chasing her out the door.

Lillian's heels clicked a staccato on the polished floor as she strode back to her office. The corridor seemed narrower, walls closing in with each step. Her mind was a hive of bees, buzzing with questions and dark possibilities.

She sank into the chair behind her desk, hands resting on the smooth wood. The photo of her and Daniel smiled at her from the corner; she turned it face down. She pulled out the client files, her fingers tracing the tab of the one now gone forever. There had to be something, a note, an overlooked warning. She flipped through the pages, eyes hunting for clues.

The door chimed softly. Carla Jenkins stood there, her presence like a lifeline to normalcy. Lillian straightened, forced a smile.

"Carla, come in."

"Hey, Lillian." Carla took a seat, her gaze lingering, searching. "Something's off. Are you okay?"

"Of course," Lillian lied. The lie felt heavy on her tongue, but necessary. "Just a long day."

"You sure?" Carla pressed. Concern knit her brow, a testament to her own healing.

"Let's focus on you," Lillian deflected, clasping her hands together to still their trembling. "How have you been feeling this week?"

Carla nodded, accepting the redirection, but Lillian caught the flicker of doubt in her eyes. She would need to be more careful. Daniel's shadow loomed, and Lillian could not let it darken more than her own heart.

Lillian watched Carla's face, the lines of worry etching deeper. She spoke, each word measured.

"Carla, there's something troubling me." Her voice hardly rose above a whisper, yet it carried the weight of her dread. "A client passed away. The circumstances... they're suspicious."

Carla leaned in, her green eyes now pools of concern. "That's terrible, Lillian. But why does this worry you so much?"

"It's Daniel," Lillian admitted, her mouth dry. "I fear he may be involved."

Carla recoiled as if struck. "Daniel? But he always seemed so devoted to you."

"Appearances can deceive," Lillian murmured, her gaze falling to her clasped hands.

Silence stretched between them before Carla exhaled slowly.

"I've started seeing someone," she said, her voice gaining strength. "He's new to me, a man you recommended. We met at one of those gatherings you encouraged me to attend."

Lillian's heart thudded. She steadied her breath.

"Tell me about him," she urged, camouflaging the tremor in her voice.

"His name is Dan," Carla began, oblivious to the storm brewing inside Lillian. "Charming and attentive. He makes me feel like I'm the only woman in the world."

Lillian nodded, pressing her lips into a thin line. She scribbled a note, a pretense for composure. Inside, her thoughts raced. She needed more, but caution was key.

"Sounds like things are going well," Lillian managed, her smile strained.

"Better than I hoped," Carla said, her smile genuine and full of hope.

Lillian's mind churned with unspoken fears as she watched Carla leave, her steps light with newfound love. Alone again, she faced the truth. Daniel's web was wide, his deceit drawing in the unsuspecting. Lillian's resolve hardened. She would unravel his lies, thread by treacherous thread.

"Dark hair, intense blue eyes," Carla continued. "He's got this way of looking at you, like he sees right through to your soul."

Lillian nodded, her fingers tapping a silent code on the armrest of her chair. Daniel's image, that familiar intensity, flashed in her mind. Her pulse quickened.

"Thank you for telling me," Lillian said, her voice steady despite the turmoil inside. "It's important to share these things."

"Of course," Carla replied. "I feel safe here, with you."

"Good. Remember, I'm here for you. Always." Lillian stood up, her movements deliberate. "We'll talk more next time."

"Thanks, Lillian." Carla's smile was warm as she left, her trust in Lillian evident.

With Carla gone, Lillian sat motionless. The office felt colder now. She needed proof. She needed to protect Carla, protect them all from his snare. Her resolve was iron; she would find the truth.

Lillian flipped through the files, her hazel eyes scanning pages with clinical precision. The office was silent save for the rustle of paper and the occasional scratch of her pen as she took notes. She paused, considering the disjointed pieces of information spread across her desk. A timeline formed, each entry a stepping stone that led to an unsettling possibility.

She reached for her phone, then stopped. No, evidence first. Her thoughts were a swarm, but her movements were methodical, deliberate. She sifted through therapy notes, searching for patterns, for words repeated, for anomalies in behavior.

Her mind returned to Carla's description, the way her voice softened when she spoke of the man with piercing blue eyes. Daniel. Lillian's heart clenched, but she pushed past the emotion, focusing on the task at hand.

"Troubled past," Daniel had said. His words echoed in the quiet of the room. Too quick to dismiss, too cold. She scribbled another note, a question mark beside it.

Hours passed. Lillian's list grew, a chain of facts and conjecture. She leaned back, eyes tired but mind alert. Each client's story hinted at something darker, a subtle manipulation she had missed before. Was Daniel capable of more? She needed to know.

The clock ticked on, the second hand's rhythm a relentless reminder of the urgency of her search. She would find the truth hidden beneath Daniel's charm. For Carla, for herself, for all those who had trusted him. Her resolve was a steel thread, unwavering.

"Solid evidence," she whispered. She would build her case, piece by incontrovertible piece.

Lillian tapped her pen against the notepad, each client's name a separate enigma. She dialed, her voice even, "I'm hoping we could meet." The calls were brief; her tone, professional yet warm. She arranged the appointments with precision, an invisible thread weaving through each conversation.

In the quiet corner of a coffee shop, Lillian sat across from Ms. Thompson. The woman's hands wrapped around her cup, knuckles white. "He seemed so insightful at first," she confided, eyes darting to the door then back to Lillian. "But it felt like he was steering my thoughts, not just listening."

"Steering how?" Lillian probed gently.

"Questions that weren't just questions. Suggestions hidden inside them. My fears grew. It was subtle but...persistent." Ms. Thompson's voice trailed off.

"Thank you for sharing this," Lillian said, her gaze steady and reassuring. They parted with a hollow promise of better days.

Next was Mr. Gardner, a man with a stoic face and eyes that didn't quite meet hers. They sat in a park, his words coming in short bursts. "Felt cornered," he muttered, "like he knew things I hadn't told him. Made me doubt my own mind."

"Did he ever make you feel unsafe?" Lillian asked, her eyes searching his.

"Can't say unsafe. Just...uneasy. Always uneasy," he replied before standing up abruptly. "Gotta go."

Each story was a tile in a mosaic, the image becoming clearer, more sinister. Lillian felt the chill of understanding creep up her spine. Daniel had woven a web around them all, threads of control and influence that tightened with every session.

She sat alone at her desk late into the night, the office silent around her. Her notes lay spread out before her, a tapestry of manipulation. Patterns emerged—Daniel's fixation on control, his ability to exploit vulnerabilities with surgical precision.

The revelation struck with the force of a physical blow. She knew these people, their lives laid bare before her in confidence, and he had used that intimacy as a weapon. Fear coiled in her stomach, a serpent waking from its slumber. She understood now the gravity of the threat, the peril that Daniel posed not just to her clients, but to her, to anyone who got too close.

Her breaths came quick, short. She needed to act, the compulsion urgent and undeniable. But she would not rush. Every move had to be calculated, every piece of evidence indisputable. The stakes were too high for anything less. Daniel's facade of concern was crumbling, revealing the darkness beneath, and she would be ready to confront it with the truth.

Lillian turned the key in the lock, a soft click echoing through the empty hallway. She stepped into her office, the safe haven where she had spent countless hours helping others navigate the stormy seas of their minds. Now, it was the command center for a different kind of navigation—through the treacherous waters of Daniel's deceit.

She settled at her desk, the glow of the computer screen casting a pale light on her focused face. Her fingers danced across the keyboard, each tap a step closer to unveiling the truth. Emails sent under the guise of follow-ups with clients were actually veiled probes for information. Her inbox filled with replies, voices from the ether offering fragments, hints, whispers of Daniel's influence.

Printouts piled high beside her, timelines and cross-referenced statements that painted a damning portrait of manipulation. Lillian's hazel eyes absorbed every word, every implication. She annotated margins, circled inconsistencies, connected dots with lines of red ink.

"Patterns," she murmured to herself. "Control. Exploitation." The words fell flat in the silence, a mantra against the growing unease within her.

She paused, leaned back in her chair, and exhaled a deep breath that seemed to carry the weight of her burden. Her mind raced, yet she willed it to calm. She could not afford the luxury of panic; precision was her ally.

The phone rang, piercing the quiet. She stared at it, heart hammering, before picking up. A client's voice, hesitant on the other end, shared a story that echoed others—Daniel's charm, the feeling of being special, then the slow realization of being trapped in his web.

"Thank you," Lillian said as she hung up, her voice steady despite the turmoil inside. Each call was another thread pulled from Daniel's carefully woven tapestry, each revelation a potential lifeline for those ensnared.

Night deepened outside her window, but Lillian worked on, the moon her silent companion. She was alone but not lonely;

purpose was her company. The clock ticked away seconds, minutes, hours—time was both an enemy and an ally. She needed it to build her case, to fortify her evidence, yet it was time that Daniel might use to strike again.

A knock at the door startled her, a late-night custodian checking in. She offered a brief smile, a facade of normalcy, while her insides churned with the knowledge of what lay ahead.

"Almost there," she whispered to herself as the custodian left, the door clicking shut once more. She returned to her vigil, her watch over the lives that had unwittingly fallen under Daniel's shadow.

Lillian knew the coming confrontation would be a battle of wits and wills. She could not bring accusations borne on the wings of supposition; they would crumble against Daniel's charm. No, when she faced him, it would be with the unyielding force of truth.

As dawn's light crept into the room, Lillian finally pushed back from her desk. Her body ached for rest, but her resolve was ironclad. She would protect them all from Daniel's dangerous obsession. She would not falter. The evidence was there, growing with each passing day, and soon, she would lay it bare for the world to see.

CHAPTER 8

UNRAVELING THE TRUTH

Bethany's office was a sanctuary of calm, the soft hum of the air conditioning a steady anchor as Lillian paced the length of the Persian rug. Her curls bounced with each step, a wild contrast to the orderly shelves lined with psychology tomes.

"Daniel's not who I thought," Lillian said, halting before the mahogany desk where Bethany sat. "There's more to him, something sinister."

Bethany's eyes, deep pools of knowing, met hers. "We've seen the signs. Your clients, they could be at risk."

"Exactly." Lillian perched on the edge of a leather chair, her hands clasped tight. "We need proof, to protect them."

"His computer," Bethany suggested, a spark igniting in her gaze. "It might hold what we're looking for."

"Can we get to it?"

"Wait until he leaves his apartment. He keeps a schedule; we can use that."

"Break-in?"

Bethany nodded once, decisively. "To safeguard your clients, yes. We'll plan it out, leave no trace."

"Okay," Lillian breathed, a weight lifting. "Let's do this."

Bethany's car idled by the curb, a block from Daniel's sleek high-rise. The dashboard clock ticked towards seven. Lillian tapped her fingers, counting the seconds. Daniel would be at his kickboxing class, body glistening, eyes on the next target.

"Time," Bethany murmured.

They slipped out, crossed the street with purpose. No glances exchanged, just the shared rhythm of their intent.

The lobby was quiet, save for the soft clack of Lillian's heels. The doorman nodded, familiar with her face. They rode the elevator, a silent ascent. Third floor. The hallway stretched, doors like sentries.

Lillian's key turned in the lock, a soft click betraying entry. Inside, Daniel's world lay open.

"Quick and quiet," Bethany whispered.

Lillian nodded, moving to the study. Papers, files, receipts scattered across Daniel's desk. She flipped through them, swift, searching. Bethany rifled through drawers, her movements methodical, precise.

"Anything?" Lillian's voice was barely there.

"Keep looking."

The apartment held its breath. Fabric rustled as they shifted cushions, checked beneath furniture. Time passed, an enemy gaining ground.

"Here." Bethany held up a flash drive, plucked from the lining of a briefcase.

"Could be it."

"Could be." Bethany pocketed the find.

They replaced each item, a puzzle piece sliding back into the perfect façade. No trace, no whisper of intrusion. Just the silence of a space observed, secrets hunted.

Eyes met, a mirror of resolve. They left as they came, the door clicking shut, leaving the quiet to settle back over Daniel's hidden truths.

Lillian's fingers traced the grain of Daniel's mahogany desk, her touch light but probing. The wood felt cold, unyielding, much like the man himself. She pressed down on a knot, a blemish in the polished surface, and it gave way with a muted click. A drawer edged open, silent and slow.

"Got something," she called softly.

Bethany was at her side instantly, her presence a steady force. They peered into the shadowed recess together. Files, lined neatly, labels facing outward. Names etched in black ink, lives reduced to folders and facts. Lillian's hand hovered, then seized a file at random.

"God," her whisper barely broke the hush. "It's all here."

"Let me see." Bethany's voice held an edge, sharp with betrayal. She flipped through the pages, the rustle of paper a discordant soundtrack to their discovery.

"Profiles, notes, weaknesses," Lillian said as they absorbed the reality of Daniel's scheming. "He's been playing them all."

"Let's copy everything. We need evidence."

"Right." Lillian's nod was tight, her movements brisk as she gathered the files.

They worked in tandem, the whir of the compact printer-scanner they'd brought along punctuating the silence. Page after page, they fed Daniel's deceit into the machine, digital proof mounting with each pass.

"Once we have this," Lillian paused, her gaze meeting Bethany's, "we confront him."

"Carefully," Bethany returned the look, her eyes dark pools of resolve. "We can't tip him off."

"No," Lillian agreed, feeling the weight of their next steps. "But it ends, Bethany. It ends now."

"Agreed."

As the last file slid from the scanner, a sense of finality settled over them. They packed up, the copies of Daniel's treachery a heavy burden in their bag. They left as methodically as they had entered, ready to face whatever storm their truth would bring.

Daniel's fingers drummed an erratic rhythm on the metal table, his gaze flicking to the entrance of the coffee shop. The bell above the door jangled as Kevin Dawson shuffled in, his shoulders hunched against the weight of unseen burdens. Daniel's lips curved into a reassuring smile, one that didn't reach the cool blue of his eyes.

"Kevin, sit down," Daniel urged, gesturing to the vacant chair. "Coffee?"

"Sure," Kevin replied, his voice a mix of gratitude and weariness.

The server approached, swift and silent. Two coffees, black.

"Rough week?" Daniel probed, his tone casual.

"Like you wouldn't believe," Kevin confessed, rubbing at his temple.

"Sometimes it feels like we're drowning, doesn't it?" Daniel said, leaning forward, elbows on the table, creating a false sense of intimacy. "But you're not alone, Kevin."

"Thanks," Kevin muttered, clinging to the lifeline offered.

Daniel sipped his coffee, bitter and strong. He waited, watching the steam curl up between them, letting the silence stretch until it was taut and ready to snap.

"Kevin," he began again, his voice low, "I'll be frank. We've both been... compromised."

"Compromised?" A frown creased Kevin's forehead.

"Some people might be digging. Looking for dirt," Daniel continued. His eyes locked onto Kevin's, unblinking.

"Dirt?" Kevin's hand trembled against his cup.

"Information can be twisted, used against us," Daniel pressed. "We need to protect ourselves."

"Protect? How?" Confusion clouded Kevin's brown eyes.

"By staying ahead. By clearing any... misunderstandings before they arise." Daniel's words were precise, each one chosen with care.

"Are you saying I did something wrong?" Kevin's voice held an edge of panic.

"Did you?" Daniel challenged, a slight tilt to his head.

"No," Kevin protested, but doubt flickered in his eyes.

"Good. But others might not see it that way. We need to make sure our stories align," Daniel said, offering a conspiratorial glance.

"Align?" Kevin echoed, the word foreign on his tongue.

"Trust me," Daniel murmured, reaching across the table to clasp Kevin's hand. "I'm here to help you, but you must follow my lead."

"Okay," Kevin nodded, though his hesitation hung in the air, a silent specter at the table.

"Remember, we're in this together," Daniel reassured, releasing Kevin's hand as the server returned to clear their cups.

"Right," Kevin agreed, standing alongside Daniel, but his voice trailed off, lost amidst the hum of the coffee shop.

They parted with a handshake, Kevin's grip uncertain. Daniel watched him leave, a predatory satisfaction settling over his features. He had planted the seeds; now he would wait for them to take root, to grow into the fear and doubt he needed to control the narrative.

With every step Kevin took away from the table, away from the truth, Daniel's desperation waned, replaced by the familiar thrill of the game.

Lillian sat across from Bethany in her dimly lit office, a list of names between them. Each one, a life Daniel had touched, twisted to his own ends. They parsed through the stories, connecting dots that formed a chilling constellation of his deceit.

"Every account mirrors the others," Bethany said, tapping a finger on the grainy wood. "He preys on vulnerability."

"Like a wolf," Lillian murmured, her mind a whirlwind of betrayal and resolve. She clutched the copies of the files, proof of Daniel's treachery, tight in her hands.

Night fell as they worked, and soon enough, the moment to confront Daniel arrived. The air was cool, carrying the weight of impending storms as Lillian approached him. His apartment loomed, a monolith of secrets she once found sanctuary in.

"Daniel," she said, her voice steady despite the turmoil within. He turned, those piercing blue eyes finding hers, a mask of innocence already in place.

"Hey, love. What's wrong?" His tone, feigned concern.

She held up the evidence, papers that screamed of his guilt. "This. This is wrong."

He took a step closer, reaching out. "Lil, you're confused. You've got this all mixed up."

The gaslight flickered in his words, trying to blur her reality. But she stood firm, the truth her shield. "I'm not confused, Daniel. I see you now."

A veil lifted from her perception, each denial from his lips only reinforcing what she knew to be true. Her hazel eyes, once warm with affection for him, now blazed with the fire of someone scorned, someone awakened.

"Look at these," she insisted, thrusting the papers toward him. "How can you deny it?"

"Paperwork? Clients? It's all explainable, Lillian. You're seeing shadows." His hand brushed hers, a move once soothing, now repellant.

But she didn't waver. "No more lies, Daniel. I'm done."

He retreated, a smile playing at his lips, a predator cornered but not defeated. "You think you have me figured out?"

"Better than you ever did," she replied.

His laughter was hollow, echoing off the walls that once whispered secrets. Lillian turned away, her heart heavy but her path clear. She would no longer be a pawn in his games. And with Bethany at her side, she would bring him to justice.

Lillian's hands trembled, the papers heavy as lead in her grip. Bethany's hand found her shoulder, a steady presence. "You're not alone," she said.

"Feels like it sometimes," Lillian whispered, the weight of betrayal a tangible thing.

"Daniel can't hurt you anymore. We have proof." Bethany's voice was firm, the timbre reassuring.

"Proof." The word felt strange on Lillian's tongue, foreign yet empowering. She met Bethany's gaze, found conviction there.

"Your clients trust you. You owe it to them—and to yourself—to end this."

Lillian nodded, the haze of doubt clearing. She had been Daniel's victim but also his adversary, stronger than he knew.

"Let's take this to the police," Bethany suggested.

"Police." Another word that echoed with finality. A nod was her reply, her resolve hardening.

They sat, side by side, mapping out their next move. A detective's name surfaced, one with a reputation for unwinding webs of deceit.

"Tomorrow," Lillian said. "We meet him tomorrow."

"Tomorrow," Bethany agreed.

The pact was set, their course charted. Together, they would dismantle Daniel's facade, brick by lying brick.

The morning sun had yet to chase away the chill when Lillian noticed it—the faintest scratch on her door lock. Her pulse quickened. They hadn't been careless; Daniel's desperation was showing.

"Look," she said, pointing out the mark to Bethany.

Bethany leaned in, examining the scratch with a clinical detachment. "He's trying to scare us."

"Or worse." Lillian's voice was steady, but her hands betrayed her, a slight quiver as she pulled her coat tighter around her.

"Let's go," Bethany urged, her eyes scanning the street for any sign of Daniel.

They walked briskly, the city waking up around them. At the precinct, they were ushered into a small room, the hum of fluorescent lights overhead. Detective Abrams sat across from them, his face unreadable behind a pair of wire-rimmed glasses.

"Ms. Carter, Ms. Wilson," he greeted, nodding at each in turn.

"Detective," Lillian acknowledged. She placed the folder on the table, its contents meticulously organized, each piece of evidence a silent testament to Daniel's treachery.

"Here's everything," Bethany added, pushing the folder toward him. "Bank statements, emails, recordings."

Abrams flipped through the documents, his movements deliberate. "You've been thorough."

"Daniel Moore is dangerous," Lillian said, her words clipped. "He's hurt people. He will again."

"His clients..." Bethany started, then paused, collecting herself. "They don't know they're victims."

Abrams looked up from the folder, his gaze meeting Lillian's. "I can see you've both been affected by this man. But you've done good work here."

"Will it be enough?" Lillian asked, the doubt creeping in despite her conviction.

"It's more than enough." Abrams closed the folder, a finality in the gesture. "We'll move quickly."

"Thank you," Bethany said, relief coloring her tone.

"Thank you," Lillian echoed, allowing herself to feel a flicker of hope.

As they left the precinct, Lillian felt the weight on her shoulders lighten ever so slightly. Bethany was beside her, a constant presence. Together, they had taken a step toward something resembling justice. It was a good feeling, fleeting but good.

Sunlight waned as they stepped out onto the street. The city's pulse thrummed beneath their feet, an undercurrent of life that now mirrored the resolve hardening within them. They walked in step, shoulders square, heads held high. Lillian's heart beat with a newfound rhythm, syncopated with purpose and determination.

"Feels like we've finally done something real," Bethany said. Her voice was steady, a contrast to the chaos that had churned around them for weeks.

"Real and right," Lillian replied. The words were simple, yet they carried the weight of their journey, a path littered with deception and pain. The air felt crisper, the future less shrouded.

They reached Bethany's car, its black paint gleaming under the glow of the streetlights. The door closed with a definitive thud behind Lillian as she settled into the passenger seat. Bethany started the engine, the rumble a quiet promise of the road ahead.

"Daniel won't know what hit him," Lillian murmured, her gaze fixed on the rearview mirror as if she could already see the fallout reflected there.

"Let him be blindsided," Bethany said, pulling away from the curb with a smooth acceleration. "He deserves nothing less."

A silent accord passed between them, an understanding that words could only diminish. They would face Daniel together, armed with truth and unyielding courage.

Lillian turned her head, watching the precinct shrink in the distance. She thought of Detective Abrams, of the folder heavy with evidence, of the countless lives twisted by Daniel's hands.

"Ready for this?" Bethany asked, her dark eyes flickering to Lillian before returning to the road.

"More than ever," Lillian answered, feeling the pieces of herself lock into place. She was no longer just a therapist, a girlfriend, a victim. She was an agent of change, a force to be reckoned with.

Bethany nodded, a small smile playing on her lips. They drove on, the city lights blurring into streams of gold and red. The night held no fear for them now, only the promise of retribution and the end of Daniel's reign over those he'd sought to control.

CHAPTER 9

BREAKING POINT

Lillian held the stack of papers with a trembling hand. The printouts, photos, and scribbled notes formed a mosaic of betrayal on the coffee table between them. Daniel leaned back on the couch, a smirk tugging at the corner of his lips.

"Paranoid again, Lillian?" His voice was smooth, almost soothing, but it carried an edge that scraped against her resolve.

"Daniel, these things don't add up." Her words came out steady, despite the chaos swirling within her. "There's too much here to ignore."

He waved a dismissive hand. "You're seeing shadows, Lillian. That mind of yours, it plays tricks."

She straightened, pressing the evidence closer towards him. "Bank statements. Messages. Dates and times that contradict each other. It's not just in my head."

"Stress," he said. "It's getting to you. You work too hard, care too much. It wears you down."

"Stop it." Her calm facade cracked, her voice sharpened by a mix of frustration and desperation. "This is real. Tell me it isn't."

He looked at her then, those blue eyes trying to pierce into her, to rearrange the truth. But she held his gaze, her hazel eyes not backing down.

"Look at these," she insisted, pointing to a photograph, an email. "Explain them."

"Explanations won't help," Daniel replied, his tone softer now, almost pleading. "Trust me, instead."

"Trust?" The word hung heavy in the air, soaked with irony. "That's what this is about."

"Exactly," he said, reaching for her hands, but she pulled away.

"Answers, Daniel. I need answers." Her heart hammered against her ribs, her breaths shallow. She needed to know. She had to know.

Daniel leaned back, his expression morphed into one of concern that didn't quite reach his eyes. "Lillian, you're doing it again," he said softly. "You take a puzzle and you twist the pieces until they fit your narrative."

"No, these pieces are real, Daniel." Her voice trembled, betraying her. "They're facts."

"Or interpretations," he countered, crossing his arms. "You interpret stress as conspiracy."

She hesitated, the seeds of doubt already sown. "But the inconsistencies—"

"Are life, Lillian. Life is inconsistent." His tone was gentle, almost caring. "But you see malice where there's none."

Her mind raced, thoughts tangled like a ball of yarn clawed at by too many cats. She wanted to believe him, to release this knot in her chest that tightened with every breath.

"Remember last month?" he continued. "You thought your phone was bugged. It was just a glitch."

"That was different," she insisted, but less firmly this time.

"Was it?" He stepped closer, his presence enveloping her. "Or is this part of the pattern?"

"Pattern?" The word echoed in her mind. Was there a pattern?

"Your need to find drama, to be the caretaker." He reached out, and this time she didn't pull away. His touch was warm, familiar. "It's why you're so good at your job. But sometimes, you carry it into our home, our life."

She searched his face for signs of deceit, for the cracks in his story, but his gaze was steady, his jaw set in earnest appeal. Her heart ached, yearning to slip back into the comfort of his assurance.

"Daniel, I—" She stopped, unmoored. "I don't know what to think."

"Think about us," he whispered. "About love."

"Love shouldn't be built on lies," she murmured, almost to herself.

"Who says they're lies?" He pulled her close, his scent enveloping her, a mix of cologne and something darker she couldn't place. "Maybe they're just misunderstandings."

"Maybe," she echoed, the word hollow. She rested her head against his chest, listening to the steady beat of his heart, wondering if its rhythm was just another deception.

Daniel walked into the bar. The lights were low, casting long shadows across the scarred wooden floor. He saw Mason Harper in a booth at the back. Daniel slid into the seat opposite him. No greetings exchanged.

"Harper," Daniel said.

"Moore." Mason's voice was cool, his gaze steady.

"Got your message," Daniel continued. "Sounds urgent."

"Your games," Mason began, leaning forward. "They're ending."

"Games?" Daniel kept his voice even. A flicker of annoyance

crossed his features.

"Come on, Daniel." Mason's tone was sharp. "The evidence is piling up."

"Is it?" Daniel asked.

"Photos. Transactions. Testimonies. They talk."

"Talk can be cheap," Daniel replied.

"Not this time." Mason's eyes didn't waver. "Not when lives are at stake."

"Whose lives?"

"Think about Lillian," Mason said.

Daniel's jaw tightened. "Leave her out of this."

"Can't do that." Mason leaned back. "She's in too deep."

"Then what do you propose?"

"Simple," Mason said. "Stop now, or else."

"Or else what?"

Mason stood up and tossed a manila envelope onto the table. It landed with a soft thud. "See for yourself."

Daniel watched him walk away. He reached for the envelope, hesitated, then pulled it close.

Daniel's fingers curled around the manila envelope, his pulse a thrumming undercurrent of fear and anger. He let out a measured breath, willing an air of control into his voice.

"Harper," he started, eyes fixed on Mason's retreating back. "There's room for negotiation."

Mason paused, half-turned, a silhouette against the dim glow from the bar. His gaze appraised Daniel, unyielding.

"Negotiation?" The word hung between them, skeptical.

"Listen," Daniel pressed, the desperation seeping through his crafted composure. "I've been resourceful, haven't I? We could use that. Together."

"Resourceful?" Mason's lips twisted into a faint, humorless smile. "You mean your talent for ruining lives?"

"Hyperbole doesn't suit you," Daniel shot back, his cool facade cracking at the edges. "We're in the business of give and take. People were happy to give, weren't they?"

"Under false pretenses," Mason returned to his seat, his posture rigid. "You took advantage of their trust."

"Trust is a currency," Daniel argued, leaning forward, his blue eyes narrowing. "An exchange. I'm offering you a partnership. Think of the success we could build."

"Success?" Mason scoffed, his voice low and controlled. "At what cost? You've crossed lines, Daniel."

"Lines are subjective." Daniel's hand twitched on the table, betraying him.

"Consequences aren't." Mason's voice was flat, final. His hazel eyes held a steely resolve that sent a chill down Daniel's spine.

"Think about it, Mason. Really think." Daniel pushed, words tumbling with urgency. "We can spin this. We can—"

"Enough," Mason cut him off. He stood again, towering over the table. "Your time is up."

"Is it?" Daniel's question was a challenge, a last-ditch effort to regain his footing.

"Your actions have consequences. You won't escape them," Mason stated. There was no inflection in his voice, just an unwavering certainty.

"Everyone escapes something," Daniel muttered, but his confidence waned, the words sounding hollow even to him.

"Goodbye, Daniel." Mason turned, leaving him with the heavy weight of silence and an envelope full of truths he wished to evade.

Left alone, Daniel sat motionless as the tension in the air slowly dissolved, replaced by the looming specter of inevitability.

The phone's shrill ring cut through the silence of Lillian's office. She hesitated, then grabbed it, her hand steady despite the tremble in her breath.

"Daniel," she answered.

"Lillian, listen," he rushed out, his voice a frantic whisper wrapped in static. "It's not me. It's Mason, he—"

"Slow down." She pressed the receiver tighter against her ear, needing to catch every syllable. "Start from the beginning."

Daniel exhaled, a gust of wind into the phone. "Mason's twisting things. He wants you to doubt me."

"Is that so?" Skepticism edged her tone.

"Believe me," he pleaded. "I'm the victim here."

"Victim?" The word tasted sour on her tongue. "You need to explain, Daniel."

"Can't you see? He's playing us both." His words tumbled over each other, desperate, urgent.

"Playing us?" She leaned back in her chair, the leather creaking under her shift. "Or just you?"

"Dammit, Lillian, this isn't a game!" His voice cracked, and for a moment, she glimpsed the man behind the mask.

"Then tell me the truth," she insisted.

"Truth," he echoed, as if the concept was foreign. "Mason's setting me up. He's jealous... envious of what we have."

"Envy can be poisonous," she said, cold logic seeping through her warmth.

"Exactly," he seized the word like a lifeline. "That's why he's doing this."

"Or maybe he's opening my eyes," she countered.

"Your eyes are open enough," he snapped, then softened. "Lillian, please."

"Daniel," she sighed. "Every answer you give, more questions follow."

"Questions can wait," he deflected.

"Can they?" Her heart raced, but her voice remained level.

"Trust me," he said, and it was almost a whisper.

"Trust," Lillian repeated, her hazel eyes staring blankly at the wall. "A currency, you said."

"Did I?" There was a pause, heavy with realization.

"Lines are subjective, consequences aren't," she recited, the echo of his own words.

"Who told you that?" A hint of fear crept into his voice.

"Someone who saw through you," she replied, the line humming with tension.

"Please, Lillian..." His voice trailed off.

"Goodbye, Daniel." She placed the receiver down with a click that seemed to echo in the empty room.

The phone lay silent on the table between them. Lillian's breath was steady, a metronome to the thrumming in her head. Daniel's eyes, those deep pools of blue that once promised oceans of safety, now seemed shallow and tinged with desperation.

"Listen," he started, his voice a forced calm. "You know how you get sometimes."

Her fingers curled into her palm, nails pressing crescents into flesh. She knew that tone, the feigned concern laced with an undercurrent of control.

"Get how, Daniel?" The question was flat, almost curious.

"Overwhelmed," he said quickly. "With your clients, your own stuff. I worry about you, that's all."

"Is that it?" Her gaze didn't waver.

"Of course." He reached across the table, trying to capture her hand. "I'm here for you, Lil."

She withdrew before he could touch her, the space between them filling with unspoken truths. His gaze flickered, then hardened.

"Things have been tough lately," he continued, pushing forward. "And maybe I haven't been perfect. But who is? We can get through this together."

"Can we?" Lillian's voice betrayed nothing of the war inside her.

"Damn it, yes!" Daniel slammed his fist on the table. "Don't let Mason or anyone else get into your head. You're stronger than that, aren't you?"

"Strength," she murmured. "Sometimes it means knowing when to step back."

"Step back?" He recoiled as if struck. "From us?"

"From everything." She stood, chair scraping back sharply. "To see clearly."

"See what?" His plea was edged with panic now.

"Truth." The word hung heavy in the air.

"Without me, you—" he began, but she held up a hand.

"Stop, Daniel." Firm, decisive. "I need time. Space."

"Space?" His voice cracked. "You mean a break?"

"Yes." It was a whisper, but it landed like a verdict.

"Please, Lil..." He was on his feet now, reaching for her again.

"No." She stepped away, out of reach. "Goodbye, Daniel."

She turned, leaving him standing there, a man drowning in shallow water. The door closed behind her with a quiet finality.

Daniel paced the length of his study, each step a measure of his fraying nerves. His sanctuary of deceit now felt like a prison. He scanned the room—every book, every forged letter, every stolen trinket—a mosaic of lies. He could hear Lillian's accusations in the silence, her words echoing off the walls. The silence was a jury, delivering its verdict with each tick of the clock.

"Escape," he whispered to the empty room. His breath fogged the glass as he peered through the window into the night. There must be a way out. He needed a plan. His mind raced, thoughts disjointed. Money. Contacts. A new identity. Panic clawed at his throat, but survival instinct pushed him forward.

Meanwhile, in the comforting embrace of her friend's living room, Lillian found herself surrounded by understanding faces. Her colleagues, no, her friends, formed a circle of trust—a fortress against her turmoil. She recounted the details, her voice steady despite the storm inside.

"He makes me doubt," she said, her hands folded tightly in her lap. "My thoughts, my memories, my sanity."

"Gaslighting," one friend offered with a nod. Another reached across the space, a silent gesture of solidarity.

"Patterns," Lillian continued. "Once invisible, now clear." She spoke of changes in Daniel, the hidden slips in his mask. They listened, their nods slow, deliberate.

"Strength in numbers," a voice chimed from the circle. They shared stories, similar battles fought alone and together. Wisdom flowed between them, a river of shared experiences.

"Protect," Lillian resolved. Her clients, her peace, herself. The word was a shield, a commitment etched in the air.

"Act," another friend urged. "Before he does."

"Truth," Lillian echoed. It was a beacon now, guiding her through the fog Daniel had cast around her heart.

"Plan," they agreed. Strategy formed from collective resolve. They would stand with her, a phalanx against manipulation.

"Thank you," Lillian breathed, her eyes reflecting the strength borrowed from her friends. Together, they would face the coming storm.

Lillian stood by the window, the night pressing its cold face against the glass. Her silhouette blurred as she traced a finger down the condensation, drawing an aimless path. She turned from the dark outside, back to her own shadow-filled room.

Her phone lay on the table, a silent sentinel awaiting Daniel's next move. It would ring, she knew. When it did, what words would spill out? Truth or more lies?

She sat at the table, the wood grain rough beneath her palms. The chair creaked, a small protest in the stillness.

A text message broke the silence—Daniel. Her heart hitched; she read the words. Promises and pleas mingled with accusations. Mason's name surfaced like a warning buoy in a treacherous sea.

"Stop," she murmured, her voice a ghost in the quiet. She wanted to believe him, to find the man she loved behind the veil of deceit. But shadows clung to his every word, a darkness that seemed to grow with each passing moment.

The phone buzzed again, insistent. She let it dance alone on the table, its vibrations a dull drumbeat against the wood.

"Time," she whispered to herself, a mantra to hold back the tide of emotion. She needed space to think, to breathe. Her mind spun with questions, each one echoing louder than the last.

"Who are you, Daniel?" The question hung in the air, unanswered. She thought of her clients, their trust placed gently in her hands. She could not falter now.

The phone fell silent, the screen dark. Lillian rose, her movements deliberate. She crossed the room to the mantel and picked up a photo—the two of them, smiles bright and unburdened by doubt.

"Enough," she said, placing the frame face down. Her decision weighed heavy, but clear. Distance would bring perspective, the kind that only solitude could offer.

She looked once more at the phone, then switched it off, severing the line that tethered her to the uncertainty. For now, the questions would remain, the truth elusive.

Lillian wrapped her arms around herself, holding tight to the resolve that had formed in the company of her friends. She would find a way through this labyrinth, clinging to the hope that daylight waited beyond the night's reach.

The sound of a door shutting softly in her heart—a pause in the rhythm of her life with Daniel. The future loomed uncertain, a canvas yet to be painted with the colors of truth and deception.

CHAPTER 10

REVELATION AND REJECTION

Lillian's fingers raced across the keyboard, her breath shallow. Her search through Daniel's files was methodical, a silent mantra of clicks and scrolls that echoed within the stillness of their shared apartment. The cursor blinked, a lone sentry amidst a sea of digital secrets.

A folder marked "Personal" caught her eye, hidden amongst mundane documents and benign clutter. The irony was not lost on her as she delved into its contents. Client names, intimate details, financial records—all laid bare in cruel black and white. Evidence of Daniel's betrayal compiled with meticulous care.

"Find something interesting?"

Daniel's voice sliced through the silence, his presence looming behind her. Lillian spun around, the laptop clutched in her arms like a shield.

"Your work," she said, her voice a blade of clarity. "It's not just your work."

His blue eyes met hers, searching for a crack in her armor. She held the evidence aloft, the folder now tangible proof of his duplicity.

"You used my trust. You preyed on them," she accused, the words chiseled from the stone of her resolve.

"I can explain," he started, but Lillian cut him off with a raised hand, the fire in her gaze unyielding.

"Save it. I've seen enough."

Daniel's knee hit the carpet with a soft thud, his movements practiced and smooth. He reached inside his jacket, producing a small velvet box that caught the light with a promise of something more, something better. His blue eyes, once an ocean to drown in, now seemed shallow, murky.

"Look at this, Lillian," he said, voice trembling like a leaf in the wind. The lid flipped open, revealing a diamond ring that glinted mockingly in the tense air between them. "Please, I'm begging you. I can change."

Lillian watched, unmoved, her heart encased in a layer of ice that his words could not melt. Her gaze was unflinching, her stance firm. She took a deliberate step back, the distance between them widening like a chasm that no jewel could bridge.

"Daniel, stop," she said. Her voice was a low whisper, but it carried the weight of mountains. "Just stop."

He looked up at her, the charm in his eyes giving way to desperation. But Lillian saw through the act, through the sheen of false tears and quivering lips. The man before her was a mirage, one that had lured her into a desert of deceit.

"Your promises are empty," she continued, each word measured, precise. "I see you now. Clearly."

Daniel's hand, still holding the ring, trembled visibly. But his grand gesture was met with nothing but the echo of his own hollow words. Lillian turned away, leaving the sparkle of false hope behind, stepping forward into a future devoid of his shadows.

Lillian stood rooted, her silhouette framed by the fading light of the evening. Her voice cut through the stillness of the room, firm and unyielding.

"Daniel, listen to me," she said. "I can't accept this. I won't."

He rose slowly, the velvet box now a lead weight in his hand. His face twisted into an expression that danced on the edge of anger and fear.

"Isn’t this what you want?" Daniel's words clung to the air, desperate. "A life together, Lillian?"

"Built on what? Your deceit?" Lillian's eyes held a depth of resolve that seemed to pierce through him. "No, Daniel. I deserve honesty. I deserve respect."

He took a step forward, his plea breaking through his usual composure. "I can give you that. I'll do anything."

"Anything but the truth," she countered and turned away, the finality of her movement speaking louder than any shout.

"Please." The word was a crack in the veneer, a break in the dam of his cultivated control.

Lillian paused at the door, not looking back. "Goodbye, Daniel."

With each step she took, the space filled with the heavy silence of truths unspoken and chances shattered. Daniel stood alone, the ring forgotten, as the door clicked shut behind him.

The door shut with a click. Lillian's feet carried her back to the center of the room, the distance from Daniel stretching with each step.

"Empty promises, Daniel," she said. "I'm done with them."

Daniel paced, the line of his jaw hardening. His hands clenched and unclenched at his sides. "You think you can just walk away?"

"Watch me," she replied. Her voice had no tremble. It was steel wrapped in velvet.

"Everything I did, I did for us!" His voice rose, sharp and slicing.

"Us?" Lillian shook her head. "There is no 'us.' Not anymore."

He stepped closer, his shadow looming. "You owe me."

"Owe you?" She held her ground, her posture straight as an arrow. "For lies? For betrayal?"

"Betrayal?" He laughed, a cold, hollow sound. "Look who's talking about betrayal. You're betraying me now, walking out like this."

"Self-preservation isn't betrayal, Daniel." Her words were crisp, clear-cut.

"Fine," he spat, the charm evaporating from his face. "Leave, then. See how far you get without me."

"Farther than I ever did with you." Her eyes locked with his, unwavering.

"Ungrateful," he hissed. "After everything—"

"Stop." The single word was a full stop, a period ending the sentence of their relationship.

"Goodbye, Daniel." She turned, her steps deliberate as she left him standing alone, the venom of his last words dissolving into the growing expanse between them.

"Stop." Lillian's voice cut through the air, a clear note amidst Daniel's cacophony of desperation. She stood unwavering, her form a bastion against the tempest he wrought.

"Please." His plea hung, suspended in the charged silence. "Lil."

She did not move, her resolve a quiet sentinel. She watched him, saw the tremor in his hands, the way his blue eyes darted. Fear lived there, fear and something darker.

"Love," he started again, but she raised a hand.

"Enough." Her command was soft but brooked no argument. The room held its breath.

Daniel's face tightened. His jaw worked over words unsaid.

She turned then, the motion deliberate, the final hinge on the door closing on what they had. Her steps were measured, a metronome to the beat of a new beginning. Each footfall echoed, a testament to distance gained.

"Where will you go?" His voice was small now, reaching.

"Forward," she said without looking back. Her hand found the doorknob, cool and certain beneath her fingers. She stepped out, away from shadows, away from the man who had become a stranger, into light that promised no lies.

"Goodbye," she whispered to the empty space where love once lived. The door clicked shut behind her, a period at the end of a long, hard sentence.

The door's click echoed. Daniel stood, motionless, a statue in the empty room. Quiet filled the spaces between the ticking clock, the sounds of life outside, the absence of her presence. A single bead of sweat traced a line down his temple. He had been exposed, stripped of pretense and left bare.

In the quiet, he felt the weight of it all pressing down on him. His shoulders slumped. The walls closed in, whispers of their shared past, now tainted with his deceit. Alone, truly alone, he could no longer ignore the cost of his actions. The charm that had once been his armor lay useless at his feet.

Lillian walked, the evening air crisp against her skin. She rounded the corner to where they waited. There was Bethany, arms open, her face a mask of concern etched into kind eyes. Olivia, lips pressed tight, held a steadiness in her gaze. Carla's silhouette leaned against the car, her posture speaking volumes of silent support. Kevin's nod offered a simple but powerful acknowledgment.

"Hey," Lillian greeted them, each word a step towards healing.

"Hey yourself," Bethany replied, her embrace enveloping Lillian in warmth.

"Let's get you out of here," Olivia said, her voice firm.

Carla opened the car door, a gesture of sanctuary. Kevin placed a gentle hand on Lillian's back, a silent sentinel as she passed by.

The car drove through streets painted with the orange glow of streetlights. Inside, words were unnecessary. Their presence spoke for them, a chorus of solidarity. The city blurred past, buildings and trees merging into a watercolor of movement and change.

At Bethany's home, they gathered in the living room. Cups of tea steamed on the coffee table. Lillian sank into the couch, the cushions accepting her weight like an old friend.

"Thank you," she murmured, her gaze meeting each of theirs.

"You don't have to thank us," Bethany said. "We're here for you."

"Always," added Olivia, her hand finding Lillian's, a lifeline thrown across turbulent seas.

"Absolutely," Carla affirmed, her nod resolute.

"Indeed," Kevin's soft tone wrapped around them, a blanket of gentle strength.

They sat together, the night deepening around them. The tea cooled, but the warmth in the room grew, a fire kindled by friendship and shared resolve. They were there, each bearing their own scars, united in their support of one another.

In the circle of friends, Lillian found something she hadn't realized she'd lost: hope. It flickered, fragile as a candle flame, but alive. With it came the promise of new beginnings and the understanding that, sometimes, the end is just a different kind of start.

Mornings held a new light. Lillian noticed it as she opened the blinds, rays spilling across her therapy room. She arranged the chairs, two of them facing each other, an unspoken invitation for open dialogue. The books on the shelf were organized by theme, a silent testament to her dedication. Clients would come and go, leaving pieces of their stories, taking snippets of hope.

She worked through her days with a steady rhythm, her sessions punctuated by moments of breakthrough and understanding. Her own heart mended a stitch with each nod, each tear wiped away, each smile that crept through the pain. She journaled in the evenings, the pen gliding over paper, thoughts flowing like the ink.

Olivia visited the office on a Tuesday. She brought lunch, sandwiches wrapped in brown paper, apple slices peeking out. They ate on the small balcony, overlooking the cobblestone street below. People passed, a tapestry of lives intertwining briefly.

"Beautiful day," Olivia said, her eyes reflecting the clear blue sky.

"Beautiful company," Lillian replied, her own gaze not leaving Olivia's face.

They shared a smile, simple and true.

Weekends found them exploring. Baltimore was old and new, brick buildings standing shoulder to shoulder with glass facades. They walked through markets, fingers brushing, laughter mingling with the calls of vendors. Olivia's art filled her studio, colors bold and brave. Lillian watched her work, the brush strokes a language of passion and vulnerability.

"Stay still," Olivia would say, looking at Lillian through the frame of her hands. "You're perfect."

Nights fell softly around them. Dinner was often a joint effort, the kitchen warm with the scent of herbs and spices. They sat close, plates forgotten as they talked of dreams and fears, the future an unwritten story they were eager to tell together.

"Trust is a strange creature," Lillian mused one evening, a half-empty wine glass cradled in her hand.

"Let it tame slowly," Olivia replied, her voice a melody in the dim light.

They discovered trust, day by day. It grew, a seed nurtured by shared secrets and silent understandings. Kisses tasted of promise. Touches whispered of comfort.

Life in Baltimore unfolded, each day a petal opening to reveal the heart of the flower. Lillian thrived, her freedom a garden blooming with possibilities. Olivia was there, sunlight and soil, laughter and love. Together, they were whole, the sum of healed pasts and bright tomorrows.

Lillian closed the last file of the day, her fingers lingering on the smooth surface of the folder. The room hummed with silence, broken only by the distant sounds of the city. She leaned back in her chair and drew a deep breath. The air was heavy with the scent of paper and time.

Her gaze drifted to the window where twilight painted the sky in strokes of lavender and gold. The clients had left, carrying pieces of her strength with them. Their stories lingered, whispers of pain and hope that echoed in the walls of her office.

She stood up, muscles stretching after hours of stillness. Her journey had taught her the weight of sorrow and the lightness of healing. She walked to the bookshelf, running her hand along the spines of well-worn texts. Each one held a memory, a moment of discovery, a step toward understanding.

The phone rang. She answered, her voice steady and clear.

"Dr. Carter," the voice on the other end began, hesitant, "I heard about your work..."

"Come in," Lillian replied, "we'll talk."

She hung up and looked at her reflection in the darkening window. Her eyes were the same hazel but wiser now, tempered by trials and warmed by love. Olivia's face appeared beside hers, a smile in her eyes.

"Another late night?" Olivia asked.

"Someone reached out," Lillian said, turning from the window.

"Good," Olivia nodded. "You help them heal."

They left the office together, the door clicking shut behind them. The hallway stretched long and empty, their steps a quiet tandem on the carpet.

Outside, the city waited. Lillian's heart beat with its rhythm, her life a part of its pulse. She took Olivia's hand, their fingers interlocking with ease. They walked, not speaking, each step a testament to the journey ahead.

Lillian knew there would be more files, more voices seeking solace.

Her own experiences were a map she could offer, paths marked with caution and hope. She would continue to guide, to support, to heal.

CHAPTER 11

A NEW BEGINNING

The door burst open. Officers streamed in, their footsteps a staccato on the hardwood floor. Daniel stood, his back straight, as hands guided his wrists into cuffs. Lillian's breath hitched. The metallic click echoed, louder than the officer's steady voice.

"Daniel Moore, you are under arrest."

The words hung thick in the air, wrapping around Lillian like a chill. Her heart drummed against her ribs, a frantic Morse code of distress. She watched, a silent observer to the unraveling of a life she thought she knew. Daniel's piercing blue eyes caught hers, searching for an ally. She looked away.

Betrayal tasted like bile at the back of her throat. Relief was there too, tangled with the hurt. Daniel's charm had been a veil, and now it lay shredded at her feet. How could she not have seen? His touch that once felt warm, now left a cold imprint on her skin.

"Anything you say can be used against you in a court of law."

The officer’s voice was calm, practiced. Lillian barely heard it. Questions swirled in her mind, each one a pointed accusation at her own judgment. What else had he hidden behind those smiles that reached his eyes but never touched his soul? She realized she had been living with a stranger, his true nature a shadow that only now stretched long across the floorboards.

"Right to an attorney."

She should have known. A therapist, skilled in reading others, yet blind to the man before her. Love had been a deception, a game Daniel played masterfully. But the game was over. And as the officers led him away, his head held high, Lillian felt the first thread of a web long woven start to unravel inside her.

Bethany's hand was firm on Lillian's shoulder, grounding her as the last police car disappeared around the corner. "You're not alone," she said, her voice low and steady.

"Never were," Kevin added, his own eyes hinting at the empathy he couldn't hide. His presence was a quiet reassurance in the dim light of the living room.

Olivia paced by the window, her silhouette sharp against the fading evening. "What do you need?" she asked, turning to face Lillian with an intensity that burned bright and clear.

"Space," Lillian whispered, her voice barely carrying. "Time."

Carla nodded, understanding without words. She moved through the room, adjusting a cushion here, straightening a vase there—small acts of putting things back in order, as if by doing so, she could help mend the chaos that had erupted in their lives.

The next day, Lillian sat across from her therapist, the air between them alive with unsaid words. The office was a neutral space, beige walls, soft-spoken clock. Lillian's hands rested in her lap, fingers entwined.

"Boundaries," Lillian started, her voice gaining strength as she spoke the word. It felt like a declaration, a promise to herself more than anyone else. "I need them."

"Good," her therapist replied, nodding once. "Let's talk about what that means for you."

Weeks passed. Mornings began with meditation, a practice Lillian never thought she'd embrace. But there she was, breathing in stillness, exhaling the doubt that had pooled inside her. Work became a place of purpose again, her clients' stories reminding her of her own resilience.

She filled evenings with walks, not aimless, but directed toward the setting sun, toward the promise of another day. Carla joined her sometimes, their strides matching in rhythm and resolve.

"Feels right," Carla said one evening as they watched the sky blush with hues of orange and pink. "Moving forward."

"Doesn't it?" Lillian agreed, feeling the ground solid beneath her feet for the first time in months.

"Here for you," Kevin texted often, little reminders that echoed in the quiet moments. He understood the solace of solitude, the peace found in silent companionship.

"Paint," Olivia suggested one Saturday, brushes and colors spread before them like a feast. They painted side by side, canvases soon blooming with strokes that spoke louder than words.

"Strength," Bethany said over coffee, her gaze piercing as she looked at Lillian. "It's always been there."

"Finding it," Lillian replied, her reflection in the dark liquid showing a woman being reborn, layer by layer.

Days rolled into weeks, and Lillian's world expanded, filled with moments of self-care and revelations. She journaled at night, releasing the thoughts that crowded her mind, giving them space on paper where they seemed less daunting.

"New beginnings," she wrote one night, and believed it.

Lillian sat at the kitchen table, her journal open. The pen hovered above the page, ready to dance with her thoughts. Olivia leaned against the counter, sipping tea.

"You're doing great," Olivia said. Her voice was soft, a warm blanket wrapping around Lillian's shoulders.

"Am I?" Lillian's eyes flicked up, seeking affirmation.

"Absolutely." Carla walked in, her presence firm and reassuring. "You've come so far."

"Remember who you are," Bethany's text message read when Lillian's phone lit up. The words were a mantra, a lifeline thrown across the waves of uncertainty.

"Your strength is inspiring," Kevin's voice crackled through the speakerphone. He was out of town but never too far for support.

"Thank you all," Lillian whispered. The gratitude was a tangible thing, heavy in her chest.

"Always," they said, almost in unison.

The days unfolded with a new rhythm, punctuated by colors and shapes on canvas. Lillian painted, her strokes bold and certain where words sometimes faltered. A landscape emerged from the white, a path winding through trees, each brushstroke a step away from her past.

She wrote too. Her stories were not of Daniel but of herself, her clients, the world as she saw it now. The ink flowed, black rivers carving canyons on the page, revealing layers of herself she had forgotten or never known.

"New hobbies?" Olivia asked one evening, their hands stained with paint.

"Old ones," Lillian smiled. "Rediscovered."

"Like what?"

"Pottery. I used to love it."

"Then let's find a class."

They did. Clay spun under Lillian's fingers, cool and yielding. It was shaping something from nothing. It was control and release, both at once.

"Look at that," Carla said, marveling at the vase taking form. "It's like magic."

"Feels like coming home," Lillian replied, her heart light.

Each day brought its own small victories. Lillian savored them, tasted the sweetness of autonomy. She built her life anew, not upon the shaky foundation of Daniel's shadow, but upon the bedrock of her own making. Her friends stood beside her, not as crutches, but as fellow travelers on this journey of healing and discovery.

"Here's to new beginnings," Olivia raised her glass one night among laughter and shared glances.

"To finding joy," Lillian raised hers in return, her gaze steady and sure.

The toast was simple. The words echoed long after the clink of glasses had faded. In them was the promise of tomorrow and all the tomorrows to come.

Lillian entered the nondescript building, her steps tentative yet determined. Inside, a circle of chairs waited, each one a lifeline to someone else who understood. She took a seat, her hands folded in her lap, feeling the weight of the room's collective heartache and resilience.

"Welcome, Lillian," said the facilitator, a nod acknowledging her courage.

"Thank you," she replied, her voice a whisper swallowed by the sighs of others seated around her.

They spoke in turns, words heavy with sorrow but edged with strength. Stories unfolded, echoes of her own, and with each confession, the knot in her chest loosened. She listened, truly listened, and when it was her turn, Lillian stood up.

"Daniel was my compass," she began, her hazel eyes scanning the room, "but I've learned it pointed south." Murmurs of understanding rippled through the group. "I'm here to find true north again."

Nods came her way, affirmations of solidarity. As the meeting closed, hands reached out, not to take but to offer. They were the hands of fighters, of survivors.

In the weeks that followed, Lillian discovered boundaries—the ones she set were not walls but gates. They opened to let in light and closed to keep out darkness. And red flags? They no longer waved at her like welcoming banners; they were alarms, loud and clear.

At coffee shops, she sat alone, savoring solitude that once frightened her. When a man's smile lingered too long or his charm felt too smooth, she trusted the prickling at the back of her neck.

"Can I buy you a drink?" a suitor asked once, leaning in too close.

"No, thank you," Lillian replied, her refusal as much a shield as it was a declaration of independence.

With each "no," her spine straightened. With every solitary walk through the park, her step grew lighter. She was mastering the art of self-care, painting her life with broad strokes of self-respect and delicate dabs of joy.

"Boundaries are new to me," she confessed to Olivia one evening.

"Like pottery," Olivia mused. "You shape them. You define their limits."

"Exactly," Lillian said, her smile reaching her eyes. "And I'm finally crafting a life that's genuinely mine."

Lillian sat, legs crossed, fingers entwined in her lap. The room was quiet except for the ticking clock and her steady breaths. A photo lay on the table, its edges worn, the face of Daniel Moore smiling up at her with those piercing blue eyes.

Forgiveness felt like a distant shore. She reached for it through the fog of anger, the swell of compassion. She had loved that smile, trusted it. Now she saw the mask.

"Anger is easy," she told the empty room. "Forgiveness, that's the hard part." Her own voice startled her, a sound in the silence.

She picked up the photo, held it close. There were good memories, tender moments. They weren't all lies. But the lies were there, coiled beneath the surface like serpents in the garden.

"Daniel," she whispered, "I forgive you." The words were stones in her mouth, heavy and hard. "I forgive you, not for you, but for me." She tore the photo in half, then into quarters. Not in fury, but with purpose. Each tear a piece of pain discarded, a sliver of resentment let go. She dropped the pieces into the wastebasket. They fluttered down like broken wings.

Later, in her office, a client sat opposite her. Lillian saw the familiar shadows in her eyes, the weight of betrayal pulling at her shoulders.

"Trust yourself," Lillian said. Her voice was firm, her gaze direct. "You know more than you think."

The client nodded, a slow, uncertain movement. A story unfolded between them, words painting pictures of manipulation, of charm twisted into control.

"Boundaries," Lillian advised, her tone gentle. "They are your right, your armor."

"Isn't it lonely?" the client asked, her voice small.

"Sometimes," Lillian admitted. "But loneliness passes. Compromise your self-worth, and that stays."

The clock ticked on. They spoke of fears, of dreams. Lillian listened, her heart open. When the session ended, the client stood, her posture a little straighter, her step a bit surer.

"Thank you," she said, her eyes meeting Lillian's.

"Thank you," Lillian echoed. In the shared space of their experiences, trust bloomed like a tough, resilient flower. It was not just her client who was healing. With each connection, Lillian wove another strand into the net that was catching her too.

The door closed with a soft click. Lillian faced Daniel across the sterile visitation table. His blue eyes sought hers, once an ocean she'd willingly drown in, now just water—shallow and clear.

"Daniel," she said. Her voice did not tremble.

"Li," he began, his tone threaded with the old warmth, "I know you're hurt—"

"Stop." She held up a hand. The word was a wall. "I'm not here to revisit lies."

He leaned back, charm retreating like a shadow at noon. "Then why come?"

"Closure," she said. Her fingers gripped the edge of the table, anchoring her to this final moment.

"You think I wanted any of this?" His voice rose, a familiar dance of deflection.

"Choices were made. Consequences followed." She kept her sentences clipped, clean cuts to sever what was left.

"I love you, Li." He reached out, but she did not move closer.

"Love doesn't manipulate. It doesn't harm." Her reply was a locked door.

"Can't we—"

"No." Her denial was quiet, firm. She stood, chair scraping softly against the floor.

"Will you ever forgive me?" He looked smaller, somehow.

"Forgiveness isn't a key to your shackles, Daniel." She took a breath, felt her own strength. "It's my freedom from what you've done."

He watched her walk away, words lost in the space between them.

Outside, sunlight touched her face, warmth without demands. Friends waited. Bethany, Olivia, Carla, and Kevin—they stood like lighthouses, their smiles safe harbors.

"Ready?" Bethany asked, her arm brushing Lillian's.

"More than ever." Lillian felt her heart, steady as a drumbeat.

They walked together, laughter spilling like music. The road ahead was open, skies wide. Lillian stepped forward, each stride a note in a song of trust, love, and happiness.

Canvas stretched across the easel, a silent witness to tentative brushstrokes. Olivia's fingers swept color into form, her gaze flitting between palette and canvas. Lillian watched, the air in the studio thick with turpentine and possibilities.

"Try it," Olivia said, her voice a low invitation.

Hesitation wavered in Lillian's chest, but she stepped forward. The brush felt foreign yet familiar as she touched it to the canvas, her line trailing like a whisper against Olivia's bold declaration of hues. Their painting blended, two stories finding harmony.

"See?" Olivia's breath warmed Lillian's ear, "You're a natural."

A laugh escaped Lillian, free and unburdened. She leaned back into Olivia, her body syncing with the rhythm of another heart. Here, in the cocoon of shared silence and understanding, their intimacy blossomed—a shy bud unfurling in the light of mutual healing.

"Your turn," Lillian murmured, offering the brush back.

Olivia took it, her hand brushing Lillian's, a current passing between them. Their eyes met, holding promises no words could keep. They painted, laughter mingling with the strokes until the canvas sang with their combined joy.

The office door opened with a confident click. Lillian stepped inside, her tailored suit hugging her curves, the fabric a soft armor woven with threads of self-assuredness. Clients waited, their faces maps of the places they'd been and the journeys they sought.

She listened, truly listened, her hazel eyes pools of empathy. Her own scars, now lessons etched in memory, lent depth to her counsel. She knew darkness but chose to offer light.

"Thank you, Lillian," a client said, standing to leave, hope flickering in his eyes—a small flame nurtured by her words.

"You're welcome," she replied, her smile genuine, her spirit untethered from past anchors.

At day's end, success was not in accolades or banknotes but in reclaimed lives, including her own. Outside, dusk cradled the city, buildings silhouetted against a twilight sky. Lillian locked the office door, her steps light on the sidewalk.

Olivia waited by the car, a figure poised in casual grace. Their eyes met, worlds colliding in a glance. Lillian's heart skipped, then settled—a puzzle piece clicked into place. Together, they drove, the city lights blurring into a stream of gold.

"Good day?" Olivia asked, her hand finding Lillian's.

"Good life," Lillian answered, her voice a quiet certainty. She turned to the window, the reflection showing a woman complete, a mosaic of healed fractures.

They moved through the evening, their shared laughter a

testament to regained joy and the unwritten paths of a future bright with promise.

The car engine hummed a soft farewell as Olivia killed the ignition. Lillian's hand lingered on the door handle, her eyes tracing the familiar path to their apartment door. The night was still, save for the rustling of leaves in the gentle wind.

"Race you," Olivia said, her lips curving into a playful smirk.

Lillian's laugh was light, unburdened. "You're on."

They sprinted, two silhouettes against the urban night canvas. Breathless, they arrived at the doorstep together, a shared victory in every gasp for air.

"Always a tie," Olivia panted, grinning.

"Perfectly matched," Lillian replied, her heart still racing from more than the run. She fished for keys in her bag, the metal cool and solid in her palm.

Inside, the apartment welcomed them with silent warmth. They fell into a comfortable routine, shedding the day's remnants along with their shoes. The lamp cast a soft glow over the room, shadows dancing on the walls.

As Lillian settled onto the couch, a vibration broke the quiet. Her phone, hidden in the depths of her bag, demanded attention. She considered ignoring it, then thought better of it. Her fingers found the device, the screen lighting up with an unknown number.

"Hello?"

"Ms. Carter?" A male voice, unfamiliar and urgent.

"Speaking."

"Detective Jameson here. I'm afraid there's been a development. We need you to come down to the station."

Her pulse quickened. "What kind of development?"

"It's about Daniel."

Olivia's gaze sharpened, a wordless question. Lillian shook her head, her mouth dry.

"Can it wait until morning?" she asked.

"Best if you come now, Ms. Carter."

"Alright. I'll be there soon." She ended the call, the weight of the handset suddenly heavy.

"Is everything okay?" Olivia's concern etched lines in her forehead.

"Something's happened," Lillian said, standing with a resolve that belied her inner turmoil. "I need to go to the station."

"About Daniel?"

"Yes."

"Want company?"

Lillian hesitated, then nodded. "Yes."

Together, they left the comfort of their sanctuary, stepping out into the night where certainty faded into shadow. The city had secrets; tonight, it seemed determined to reveal one more.

CHAPTER 12

LOVE REDISCOVERED

Lillian twisted the silver ring around her finger, a habit when deep in thought. Across the table, Olivia leaned forward, elbows on the worn wood, her brown eyes locked on Lillian's.

"Ever feel like you're just skimming the surface?" Olivia asked, a lock of red hair falling into her gaze.

"Every day," Lillian confessed. "Like I'm treading water."

"Let's dive deeper then," Olivia suggested, and Lillian felt the pull of an unspoken promise between them.

They talked. Words flowed like the coffee in their cups. Dreams spilled out, fears followed, each revelation a brick removed from the walls they had built around themselves. Olivia spoke of a canvas waiting for bold strokes; Lillian shared the weight of others' secrets.

"Therapy's not just my job," Lillian said. "It's who I am. But it can be... consuming."

Olivia reached out, her fingertips brushing Lillian's hand. "You're not alone in that."

The café buzzed around them. The clink of cups punctuated their confessions.

"Daniel doesn't get it," Lillian admitted.

"More reason to find people who do," Olivia replied, her smile a silent challenge.

They lingered long after their plates were cleared. Laughter mingled with the aroma of fresh pastries. Shared interests emerged, values aligned like stars in a constellation guiding them to this moment.

"Art's my release," Olivia said. "What's yours?"

"Still searching," Lillian answered, hope flickering in her hazel eyes.

"Search together?" Olivia offered.

"Deal," Lillian agreed, sealing it with a handshake that lingered.

In the simple touch, a connection deepened, a friendship blossomed into something more. They left the café side by side, the city of Baltimore an open book before them, pages ready to be filled.

The sun was high over the Atlantic, its glare on the water sharp like shards of glass. Lillian and Olivia walked down the beach, their hands clasped, fingers woven tightly. Sand clung to their feet, and the rhythm of the waves played background to their silence.

"Beautiful," Olivia said, her words taking flight with the seabirds.

"Perfect," Lillian replied, the breeze catching her curls.

They stopped to watch the horizon, a line so clear it could have been drawn with one of Olivia's pencils. A kiss passed between them, brief but branded with promise. They moved again, leaving only transient impressions behind.

Later, the sky turned a bruised purple. They sat wrapped in a blanket, the day's warmth trapped against their skin. Lillian leaned her head against Olivia's shoulder.

"Rough week," she murmured.

"Tell me?" Olivia's voice was soft but steady.

"Another loss. Clients come and go, but some leave a scar," Lillian confessed, her eyes tracing the ebb and flow of the tide.

"Scars are just another kind of memory," Olivia said. "They shape us."

"Shape or break?"

"Your choice."

Lillian looked up, met Olivia's gaze. There was truth there, and something more—strength.

"Thank you," Lillian whispered.

"Always," Olivia answered.

The night deepened around them, but they were no longer alone. Together, they faced the dark, the pull of the ocean a reminder that everything ebbs, flows, but rarely breaks.

The gallery hummed with voices, the walls adorned with vibrant canvases that told stories in color and shadow. Olivia's pieces commanded an entire corner, a mosaic of her inner world. Lillian stood before one large painting, an abstract whirl of reds and blues clashing in a dance of chaos and harmony.

"Beautiful," Lillian said, her voice barely above the din.

Olivia, at her side, smiled, her eyes reflecting the hues of her work. "It felt right."

"Feels like a storm being tamed," Lillian observed.

"Something like that," Olivia agreed, her gaze lingering on the canvas before meeting Lillian's. "Thanks for being here."

"Wouldn't miss it," Lillian replied, her words simple but

weighted with sincerity.

They moved through the room together, Olivia sharing anecdotes behind each piece, her voice a soft thread leading Lillian through the tapestry of her artistry. Onlookers came and went, offering praise and admiration, but Olivia's attention remained anchored to Lillian's reactions, finding validation in her quiet awe.

Later, they retreated to the sanctuary of Lillian's apartment, the night outside a canvas awaiting its own set of stars. They sank into the couch, a bowl of popcorn between them, an old movie flickering to life on the screen.

"Classic," Olivia grinned as the title credits rolled.

"Best kind," Lillian agreed, tossing a kernel into her mouth.

Their laughter mingled with the on-screen dialogue, light and unrestrained. Olivia's head rested against Lillian's shoulder, a silent affirmation of trust and comfort. The movie played on, a backdrop to their shared warmth.

"Good day," Olivia murmured during a lull in the soundtrack.

"Good life," Lillian corrected, her words a gentle echo of promise.

Olivia turned, her lips finding Lillian's in the semi-darkness, a soft press that spoke louder than any dialogue. It was a brief connection, yet it held the entirety of their journey—past struggles, present joy, future possibilities—all within the span of a heartbeat.

As the credits rolled, they remained intertwined, the world pared down to the space they occupied, hearts beating in tandem with the quiet conclusion of another shared day.

Lillian led Olivia through the wrought-iron gates. The park unfolded in swathes of green and bursts of spring flowers. A secluded spot, a checkered blanket laid out with care, awaited them.

"Surprise," Lillian said, her smile tentative, hopeful.

Olivia's eyes lit up, that spark of mischief dancing within. "This is for us?"

"Only us." Lillian's answer was simple, the depth of it hanging between them.

They sat, knees touching, a basket between them brimming with foods Olivia loved. Cheese, ripe strawberries, tiny sandwiches without crusts. They ate, fingers occasionally brushing, laughter soft under the vast sky.

"Thank you," Olivia whispered, her hand finding Lillian's. "For this. For everything."

"Happy," Lillian replied, her voice steady despite the flutter in her chest.

"Happy," Olivia echoed, leaning into a kiss that tasted like strawberry and promise.

The dance studio was mirrored walls and polished floors. The instructor called, 5-6-7-8, and the music took over. Lillian was grace contained, movements precise; Olivia was wilder, joy unrestrained.

They found each other's arms, and the room fell away. Spin, step, spin again. Olivia's laughter was a melody that matched the beat. Lillian's focus was absolute, every motion a word unsaid.

"Look at us," Olivia breathed as they moved as one.

"Always," Lillian replied.

The class ended. They remained. Music played on, softer now, just for them. They danced, not for the steps or the rhythm, but for the closeness it allowed, the silent language of bodies in sync.

"Perfect," Olivia said.

"Perfect," Lillian agreed.

And they danced until the night told them to rest.

Sunlight glinted off the harbor as Lillian and Olivia wove through the throng of Baltimore's weekend crowd. Brick-lined streets led them past rows of boutiques, each window a canvas displaying the city's eclectic tastes. They paused, hands clasped, before a vendor boasting crab cakes with a secret recipe.

"Try one?" Olivia asked.

"Lead the way," Lillian said.

They ate, the flavor bold, a hint of Old Bay seasoning on their lips. Laughter bubbled up between them, easy and unforced. They continued on, steps in rhythm with the heartbeat of the city.

Further down, a jazz ensemble filled the air with sultry notes. Olivia swayed, her free spirit infectious. Lillian matched her movement, a smile playing on her lips. Music wrapped around them, a familiar comfort.

"Art is life here," Olivia said, eyes aglow as they passed murals vibrant with color.

"Your world," Lillian replied.

"Ours," corrected Olivia, squeezing her hand.

As afternoon turned to dusk, they found a bench secluded by climbing ivy. The city's hum was a distant lullaby.

"Talk to me," Olivia prompted, eyes searching Lillian's.

"About?"

"Tomorrow. The next day. Us."

The words hung, weighty with possibility. Lillian took a breath, finding courage.

"Adventures. Together."

"Mountains? Seas?" Olivia teased, but her gaze held earnestness.

"Both," Lillian affirmed. "And quiet mornings. Coffee shared, your art filling our walls."

"Love," Olivia whispered.

"Always love," Lillian echoed.

Their future unfolded in the exchange, a promise made tangible in the heart of the city that witnessed their bond. Baltimore, with its relentless energy and hidden oases, mirrored the life they planned—a tapestry of experiences, woven together by two souls who had chosen to navigate the complexities of life as one.

The sun dipped low, touching the horizon with a fond farewell as Lillian and Olivia joined the throng of townsfolk gathering in the heart of Baltimore's community square. A banner flapped gently above the stage reading, "Celebrating Local Heroes." The air was rich with the scent of sizzling food from nearby vendors and the sound of collective chatter.

"Looks like the whole town is here," Lillian murmured, her fingers intertwined with Olivia's.

"Because of you," Olivia replied, her voice steady but eyes glinting with pride.

Lillian shook her head. "Us," she corrected. They had become more than two individuals; they were a partnership, their contributions woven into the fabric of the community.

As the mayor took to the stage, a hush fell over the crowd. He spoke of growth, of nurturing hands, and artistic flair that had brushed new life into tired streets. When he called their names, applause erupted.

"Olivia Stone and Lillian Carter," the mayor announced,

beckoning them forward.

They moved through the crowd, each step an echo of their journey together. Onstage, handshakes were exchanged, and certificates pressed into their palms. Lillian's gaze caught Olivia's, the unspoken words swirling between them—this recognition was a testament to their love's power to transcend personal joy and touch others' lives.

Later, when the dusk had turned to a velvet night, Lillian stood beside Olivia in a small garden awash with fairy lights. Their loved ones encircled them, faces aglow with soft light and softer smiles. It was time for vows, but the grandeur of traditional promises seemed out of place for two hearts already so deeply entwined.

"I vow to be your harbor," Lillian began, her voice clear, "and your sail. To ground you when storms rage and to journey with you when horizons call."

"Your laughter will be my favorite song," Olivia pledged, her brown eyes locked on Lillian's. "Your dreams, my map. In art, in healing, we'll paint our days."

"Through challenges," Lillian continued, "I promise patience. Through differences, respect. Love will be our constant, our compass."

"Wherever we stand," Olivia said, "it will be home if you're beside me."

"Unconditionally," they said together, the word a shared breath that sealed their bond.

There were no grand gestures, only the simplicity of true commitment. Cheers rose up around them, the warmth of their community embracing them in a collective embrace of acceptance and admiration.

In that moment, Lillian understood the depth of their connection was not just about the love they shared, but also about the strength they offered to those around them. The world could be harsh, unpredictable, but together, they had created a sanctuary, a ripple of change that started with two souls and extended far beyond.

The dance floor shimmered. Lillian's dress swirled around her, a cascade of light. Olivia led with gentle confidence, their steps in sync. The murmur of conversations, the clinking of glasses. All fell away under the music's thrall.

"Happy?" Olivia's voice was low, a thread woven through the melody.

"Immensely." Lillian's reply was a smile, words unnecessary.

They spun. Each face in the crowd blurred into the next—friends, family, a tapestry of their lives. The room pulsed with affection, a tide rising with each beat. Lillian caught sight of her own joy mirrored on every surface, in every glance.

"Think we can sneak away soon?" Olivia's brow arched, playful.

"Let them have us a little longer," Lillian said. "We'll have forever."

Later, luggage in hand, they stood together, poised on the edge of tomorrow. A taxi waited, its engine a quiet promise. They kissed, not for the crowd that had gathered to see them off, but for themselves.

"Where to first?" Olivia asked as they settled into the back seat.

"Surprise me," Lillian said.

And so they went, wheels turning toward the unknown. Landscapes changed beyond the windows, cities giving way to countryside then back again. Each mile a memory in the making.

They walked foreign streets, Olivia's hand a constant presence in Lillian's. Markets buzzed around them, a symphony of life. They tasted exotic flavors, laughter their shared language.

At night, in the quiet spaces between one adventure and the next, they spoke of art, of healing, of the canvas of the future. Their words were few, but their meanings vast, an ocean's depth in each pause, each touch.

Olivia sketched seascapes on hotel stationery. Lillian watched, love swelling like the tides in those drawings. They were here, somewhere new, yet nothing had changed. They were home.

The key turned. The door swung open. The scent of home rushed to greet them, a blend of old books and jasmine from the vase on the windowsill. Lillian stepped over the threshold, Olivia's hand in hers.

"Back again," Olivia said, her voice a soft hum in the quiet.

"Back to start anew," Lillian replied. She dropped the keys into the bowl by the door, metal clinking against ceramic.

They moved through the rooms, sunlight pooling on wooden floors. Each step was familiar, each sight a welcome echo of days past. The walls held their shared history, silent witnesses to every tear and smile.

In the kitchen, Lillian filled the kettle. The click of the switch, a declaration of routine. Olivia leaned against the counter, arms crossed, watching. Her eyes traced the lines of Lillian's face, reading the story written there since their departure.

"Tea?" Lillian asked, already knowing the answer.

"Always," Olivia responded.

Steam rose. Cups clinked. They sat at the table, fingers touching, eyes holding fast. Talk of challenges ahead remained unspoken. There was time for that. Now was for the quiet reassurance of presence, the silent language of glances and breaths shared.

"Whatever comes," Olivia said at last, "we face it."

Lillian nodded. "Together."

Their cups were empty but they lingered. The sun began its descent, shadows lengthening across the floorboards. A cool breeze whispered through the open window, carrying the sounds of Baltimore—their city—alive and vibrant outside their door.

"Home," Lillian said, not just a place, but a truth felt deep in her bones.

"Home," Olivia echoed, her smile a promise of every day to come.

They stood, hands joined, hearts certain. Love had been a journey. Now, it was an anchor.

ABOUT THE AUTHOR

Emmanuel Simms is the creative genius behind the award-winning brand, The Clouts. What began as a simple video idea evolved into a groundbreaking concept that captured the hearts of audiences worldwide. His innovative storytelling led to the co-creation of the animated series, The Pettys, alongside Cece Peniston, the queen of house music. However, The Clouts' journey didn't stop there. A viral sensation and recipient of numerous awards, including Best Animation for The Clouts Halloween, a 15-minute comedic music spin-off, Emmanuel Simms continues to push the boundaries of storytelling, taking audiences on unforgettable adventures with his unique vision.

YOU CAN'T EAT EVERYBODY'S HUMMUS
"Change isn't just a goal. It's the path."
Emmanuel Simms
DIP INTO LIFE WITH EMMANUEL OVERTYME SIMMS

BEST
SELLER
AUDIO
HEALING
MISSION
HE AL
Empower Your Journey
By: Altamit lewis
My.EudaimoniaTv.com
MINDSET - BUSINESS - MONEY
MONEY
IN THE MIDDLE
PODCAST
Money In The Middle Podcast
Money In The Middle

EMMANUEL"OVERTYME" SIMMS
ACT LIKE A Rapper,
THINK LIKE AN
EXECUTIVE
Transform your beats into boardroom
victories: a guide for artists ready to
dominate the charts and their finances.

www.ingramcontent.com/pod-product-compliance
Lightning Source LLC
LaVergne TN
LVHW090528110826
845146LV00003B/1027

* 9 7 9 8 8 9 3 7 9 0 5 9 7 *